WRITTEN AND ILLUSTRATED BY
JANE ASHER

SILENT NIGHTS

FOR YOU AND YOUR BABY

PELHAM BOOKS

Dedicated to the memory of my father,
whose clear, concise and amusing writing
sets an example I shall always strive to follow.

First published in Great Britain by
Pelham Books Ltd
44 Bedford Square
London WC1B 3DP
1984

Asher, Jane
    Silent nights for you and your baby.
    1. Infants – Care and hygiene
    649'.122   RJ61

    ISBN 0-7207-1548-2

Typeset by MS Filmsetting Limited, Frome, Somerset
Printed and bound by
Blantyre Printing & Binding Ltd.,
London and Glasgow

CONTENTS

ACKNOWLEDGEMENTS

I would particularly like to thank Dr Miriam Stoppard, Sheila Kitzinger and Drs Andrew and Penny Stanway for talking to me about the book and for their encouragement, support and advice. I am especially grateful to Penny Stanway for reading through the manuscript and giving me her comments and for writing the foreword.

Many thanks also to my health visitor Mary Pucknell, to Flora Casement for her help with research and to the many friends and relations who gave me the benefit of their experience.

Without the encouragement and help of my husband I would certainly never have tackled the drawings and I would like to express my gratitude to him not only for his love and support but also for providing me with the three beautiful inspirations for the book: Katie, Alexander and Rory, that make all the sleepless nights worthwhile.

FOREWORD
By Dr PENNY STANWAY

'There is a time for everything,
and a season for every activity under heaven.'
(Ecclesiastes 3 v.1 NIV)

For many parents of young children the 'time' for broken nights seems too long and it's scarcely surprising that of all childcare problems, difficulty with sleep heads the list.

Jane Asher writes from experience and with intelligence and wit as she explores how to cope with sleeplessness and broken sleep. She reminds us that if nothing works, a good laugh can put everything into perspective and make the situation bearable. The amusing pictures she paints of her own night-time antics will be enough to lighten the mood of many a tired parent.

What makes this book special is its acknowlegement that young children often sleep far better with their mothers: a hard fact to swallow for a society which separates children and parents so much. However, the wishes and needs of the rest of the family are not forgotten and the many practical suggestions will surely help all who find this time hard.

INTRODUCTION

1 am Rory (4 months) wakes for a feed. Stagger across the room to his carrycot, blearily lift him out and try to get him latched on before he makes enough noise to wake Alexander (2) next door. Finish feed and settle Rory back to sleep by about 1.20.

1.40 Just beginning to drift back to sleep when Katie (10) walks in feeling very hot and miserable. Obviously she's developing the 'flu which everyone at school seems to have. Gerald (over 21) gets her some soluble aspirin and after lots of cuddles she goes off to sleep in our bed, still steaming hot.

2.30 Rory wakes for another feed – unusual but not unheard-of – my good humour beginning to fray a little. Get him back down by 3.0. Can't get back to sleep. Try to remember the dream I was halfway through when first woke. Eventually begin to doze.

3.20 Alexander shouts from next door. Normally might leave him a while to see if he would go back to sleep but tonight don't want to risk waking either of other two so Gerry goes to him. He's wide awake, standing up in the cot, beaming. Much against usual rules we bring him into our bed too, hoping he might settle back to sleep. Bound to catch Katie's 'flu but probably already got it. Silence.

4.00 'Daddy you're a cake.' Alexander's wit is rather hard to take at this hour in the morning. G and I keep eyes tight shut and pretend to be asleep.

'And Mummy's a sandwich.

'MUMMY YOU'RE A SANDWICH'

'Mummy's a very tired sandwich Alexander.'

'No you're not.'

'Yes I am. And Daddy is a very tired cake. Look — the cake's asleep. The cake and the sandwich are going to have some more sleep or they won't be able to play games in the morning.' Pause.

4.10 'I'm a tractor and I'm going to crash you. I'M GOING TO CRASH YOU. AND I WANT MY CORNFLAKES.'

Katie stirring and Rory starting to beat up for another feed so we decide to abandon the rest of the night and take Alexander downstairs for a pre-dawn breakfast.

As can be seen from this brief outline of a recent thankfully fairly unusual night in our house there can be no guarantee of peaceful nights with children of any age. Some people really do seem to produce those amazing babies who do everything by the book, slipping into convenient four-hourly feeding schedules and sleeping peacefully in between, but the three we have produced have all in varying degrees given us broken nights and worn patches in the carpet from nightly pacing.

It's strange that one of the first questions people ask about a new baby is 'Is he good?' meaning of course does he sleep most of the time. The idea that a little baby can be 'good' or 'bad' is a very odd one in any case, and so many of the 'problems' of children and young babies are more as a result of the way our society expects them to behave, rather than from any inbuilt 'naughtiness'. In a more natural society our babies would be constantly at our side, waking frequently in the night to feed and never expected to sleep alone in a dark silent room for hours at a stretch. However, given the way we have organised our lives we obviously have to gently encourage our babies to sleep through the night and there are many ways of doing this from an early age that are worth trying before any serious 'problems' set in.

Most of this book is concerned with newborn and very young babies, and will hopefully be useful in a preventive way, but I have included a section on older babies and toddlers with some hints on the sort of 'retraining' that may be necessary if you are having trouble at night. Unless you are an extraordinarily calm and patient person a wakeful toddler can be a very disruptive influence in the household. I read an article recently on children who wake in the night which included the sentence: 'You may even feel a sort of anger well up inside you as you are called yet again into his room'. *May*! *SORT OF!!* Obviously whoever wrote that has never experienced a wakeful child at 3 am!

There is considerable recent evidence to show that a difficult birth or even certain factors during pregnancy can affect the way a baby sleeps later on, and if your baby has difficulties at night it is much less likely to be due to your handling of him than was previously thought. People whose babies sleep easily and lengthily don't understand this and can be very unsympathetic.

I have referred to the baby as 'he' throughout the book because as our two last children have been male I tend to think of them when writing about babies in general, and it is less clumsy than continually referring to 'he or she'.

Nowadays both parents are usually keen to share in every aspect of babycare and apart from breastfeeding and the limitation of time at home due to one or both having to be out at work there is of course no reason why both mother and father shouldn't take on any of the duties involved in looking after young babies. This book is addressed to either or both parents or to any other person bringing up a baby.

Our third baby, Rory, is so far proving to be the best sleeper of the three, perhaps partly due to hard-learnt lessons with the other two, and I hope this gathering together of our experiences plus ideas picked up from friends, research and other parents will be useful and reassuring to anyone caring for a young baby. I am lucky enough to have help with Rory during the day, which has given me the time to write this book between the demands of the rest of the family and small excursions into my other work.

I do sometimes wonder if my husband and I are too soft on the children: one of Alexander's favourite games at the moment is for me to pretend to be a little boy who keeps calling for his mummy at night. He is the mummy, and when I call he marches straight up to me and says 'I'm going to hit you on the head with a hammer.' Perhaps he should have written the book....

FEEDING

BREAST OR BOTTLE?

It has always seemed to me unfair that on the whole bottle fed babies sleep longer between feeds than breast-fed ones, and that they tend to go through the night earlier. There can be no question that if you want to give your baby the best possible start you will breastfeed him for as long and as fully as possible and it would be far more just if nature would reward you with the sleep you long for during the first few exhausting weeks. Not that bottle-fed babies are all good sleepers – far from it – but cows' milk certainly takes longer to digest and so generally keeps them feeling full for longer stretches. Another advantage of bottle feeding is that it means both parents can share equally the night feeds, but even if the baby is breastfed the father can help get him back to sleep or do the nappy changes. Many fathers nowadays want to join in as much of the baby care as possible, and the more these difficult early nights are shared the closer will be the bond between all members of the family.

Whether breast or bottle fed the first few weeks must be devoted to feeding whenever the baby wants it, which in my case with all three children seemed to be almost constantly, particularly in the evenings.

I felt more and more like a dried prune and the babies looked like Michelin men, but I have always felt instinctively, and there is increasing evidence to support it, that you cannot overfeed a baby if you are breastfeeding. Alexander put on weight very quickly in the first few weeks – and as a nine-pounder he had hardly been a bantam-weight to start with – and when I took him to be weighed at the clinic I used to get a few raised eyebrows. Luckily there was one lady doctor there who backed me all the way: she had worked extensively abroad, and told me that the Samoan women used to carry their babies at the breast and let them feed whenever they wanted which was almost constantly. This produced big balloons of babies, but they all grew up into beautiful tall slim adults. I can't pretend Alexander is exactly slim at $2\frac{1}{4}$ but he's getting nicely into proportion now. When I look back at some early pictures of Katie I am amazed how podgy she was too at eight months or so – now she is a very slim, not to say skinny, ten-year old. Bottle feeders may have to be a little more careful, it can be harder to lose the weight put on by cows' milk.

It is very important in these early days to snatch sleep whenever and wherever you can, for unless you happen to have one of the very unusual babies who settle quickly into a four or five hour pattern, the nights will be very broken indeed. At this stage the only attitude to have is to GO WITH IT – DON'T FIGHT IT. Accept that sleep will be achieved in short bursts rather than the long stretches you are used to and it will be far less frustrating and worrying.

DAY AND NIGHT

Even when he is very young there are ways of helping the baby to start to differentiate between day and night, and the way you feed him should be geared to this. Whether he sleeps in your bed or his own cot (see 'Environment') make sure that the night feeds can be given as quickly and quietly as possible preferably without putting a light on or making a lot of noise. If breastfeeding, wear a nightdress or pyjamas that open easily at the front, as fumbling with difficult buttons while holding a starving impatient baby can be very frustrating and it's much better and more relaxing for everybody that he should be able to get to the milk as soon as he wakes and without having to cry. For bottle feeders make sure that everything is at hand and that enough feeds are prepared to see you through the night.

Unfortunately not all babies will feed thoroughly and quickly until full and then settle peacefully into sleep – often the baby seems to have had plenty but will wake for a little 'top up' a few

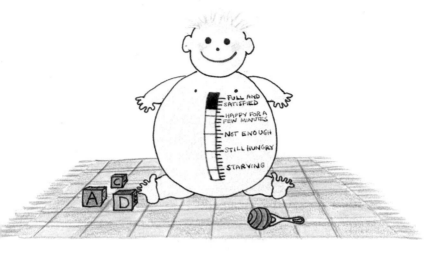

FULL AND SATISFIED

HAPPY FOR A FEW MINUTES

NOT ENOUGH

STILL HUNGRY

STARVING

'If only babies had a sort of milk gauge to show how full they were.'

minutes later. If only babies had a sort of milk gauge to show how full they were one would know whether to slip back into a deep sleep or hover around waiting for the final fill up. Equally some babies will need burping during and after a feed while some will settle quite happily without. Only experience of your own baby will tell you which sort he is. (See 'Discomfort.')

There is no need for a young baby to have anything at all other than milk, as this will give him everything he needs including enough water to quench his thirst. However, if you think you may ever want your breast-fed baby to take a bottle then it's a good idea to introduce him to one early on. With my second baby I was adamant about his having nothing at all other than breast milk and from birth onwards would not allow him to have any water, glucose etc. I did regret it, as later on when I wanted to express milk and leave it for him during the occasional evening out or break from night feeding he would have nothing to do with a bottle. With my third baby I have been far more flexible and find that the occasional drink of water, fennel or dilute fruit juice can be very useful between feeds and for getting him used to taking a bottle. I am however very much against complementary bottles of milk under six months, as even one can undo much of the good that you are doing by breastfeeding, and need hardly ever be necessary if you feed often enough to maintain a good supply. Early introduction of cows' milk or soya milk can set up allergies for life, and the results of these could prove far more disruptive to good sleep later on than keeping up the night feeds in the early stages! Tempting as it may be to leave a bottle of formula for someone else to give at night to let you have a little well earned rest this should be avoided for the first three or four months at least. Instead try expressing.

EXPRESSING

Expressing can seem almost impossible at first, but with perseverance and practice it does get easier: the secret is to take it very gently and calmly and not expect too much of yourself. When I first started trying after having Katie I couldn't believe I would ever produce any measurable amount: after perhaps ten minutes of very uncomfortable squeezing and manipulating I might find a few little drops in the bottom of the container – I couldn't bear to transfer it into a bottle as even the tiny residue left behind represented so much time and effort and there was nowhere near enough to feed her anyway. I soon gave up.

After I had Alexander I tried again with the rubber bulb and glass type of expresser but found it very uncomfortable, and as he wouldn't take a bottle anyway I didn't persevere. Now, however, since having Rory, I am quite proficient. I started by using the type of gadget that looks like a giant syringe: I found it much more comfortable and successful than the bulb one, and the only problem was how to use it in any sort of privacy. For some reason Katie and Alexander found it hilariously funny and would watch me struggling away in fits of giggles.

If you get really keen and want to leave large amounts on a regular basis then it may be worth hiring an electric pump from your local branch of the N.C.T. It's expensive but can be worth while if you need to fit in a few hours of work each week, or have a busy social life. I have hired one while I am feeding Rory: it does make you feel rather like a cow in a milking parlour but it's wonderfully easy to use and you can produce plenty of milk very comfortably. The privacy is no easier — Alexander is so fascinated by any type of machine or motor at the moment that he spotted the pump the minute I brought it in the house, and trying to relax and allow my let-down reflex to work while my every move is watched from close proximity by an eagle-eyed two-year old mechanic is not easy. He even announced in the middle of a rather quiet lunch with some friends the other day 'I want to see your breast-pump.' Quite a conversation-stopper.

Keep everything scrupulously clean and sterilised and put the milk straight into the fridge where it can be kept for three days, or once cooled can be frozen and kept for three months. Never join up small quantities of different temperatures — make sure they have been cooled in the fridge before adding one to another. My health visitor had a brilliant idea for storing it: use the Playtex plastic bottle liners which are pre-sterilised and can be slipped straight into a bottle. You don't have to use the complete Playtex system — they work perfectly well in an ordinary bottle with the top screwed down over the plastic.

When you have accumulated enough feeds in the freezer then you can ask your husband, mother or a friend to do a night for you, and even just one whole night's sleep can be an enormous boost. If you are bottle feeding then hopefully your partner will be taking his turn at the nights in any case. Sometimes the father can feel very shut out in the early days by the closeness of mother and baby, and the more he can share in the everyday (and night!) feeding and changing the more quickly his relationship with the child will grow.

GETTING BIGGER

After a few weeks, if your demand fed baby is still demanding his feeds rather more often than you may like it is worth gently starting to persuade him to go for longer periods between them. This is where his being used to a bottle pays off – when he seems hungry but has had a recent feed try offering him some water, very dilute fruit juice or a herb drink. It's much better if this can be given by Dad – the smell of milk on the mother may well start the baby clamouring for a breast feed when he could do quite well without. This applies to day or night: during the day if he learns to do without milk for longer stretches then his stomach will gradually adjust, and of course if some of the night feeds are replaced by water or juice then he may well stop bothering to wake up for them. Never let him be unhappy or hungry, this can only work against you and make everybody miserable – if he really still needs frequent feeds then he must have them. When Rory had a cold recently he went back to feeding every hour right through the night for four or five nights – just as I was beginning to despair he suddenly returned to his relatively reasonable two to three hourly ones.

SOLIDS

At about four months, or when your doctor or health visitor advises, you will start him on solids. This may or may not help the sleep pattern but tempting as it may be, the prospect of a better night's sleep is no justification for cramming the baby with as many calories as he can take. The instinctive feeling that a large late night supper will help to see him through the night is probably a false one – good satisfied sleep seems to depend more on the quantity of food taken during the day as a whole, although even with a baby just starting on solids sometimes a teaspoon of something tasty and filling at about six o'clock can make quite a difference to the night.

ALLERGIES

There is much interest in this subject at the moment, and I'm sure there is a great deal yet to be discovered about the way food affects us. Certainly many parents of so-called 'hyperactive'

'The instinctive feeling that a large late night supper will help to see him through the night is probably a false one.'

children claim remarkable improvements in them if they are put on diets free from preservatives, colourings and artificial flavourings. This sounds very reasonable: I think we may look back in amazement in a few years at the large amounts of pesticides, chemicals and so on that we all eat. If you believe your child may be truly hyperactive then do get in touch with the Hyperactive Children's Support Group.

The most commonly quoted suspect in the additive list is the orange colouring tartrazine, or colour E102 as it is usually called on a list of ingredients. This is present in most types of orange squash, among other things, which children tend to drink in great quantities. Even if your child is not hyperactive but tends to wake at night or gets fractious very easily then there's no harm in cutting out this colour to see if there's any improvement. I have removed it from our family's diet just to be on the safe side.

Sugar has also been blamed for behaviour disturbances, and as this is so very bad for children's teeth it can only be a good thing to cut it out as much as possible. We have always had a Saturdays only rule for sweets in our house and we try to save cakes and biscuits for parties and special occasions.

Many other foods have been found to cause allergic reactions in certain babies and children, and the Royal College of Physicians has recently published a report urging doctors to take the whole subject more seriously and pressing for the need for further research. If you feel your child might be reacting to a food then it may be worth writing down everything he eats until you narrow down a few suspects. Do talk to your doctor about your child and if necessary ask to see an allergy specialist.

It is often suggested that babies may be allergic to cows' milk. (See p. 16.)

THE DAY BEFORE

From a very early age the amount of time that a baby is active and stimulated during the day can affect the amount that he will sleep later. In the first few weeks sleeping and waking is fairly haphazard but even in these early stages one can help the baby to start to differentiate between day and night. Quite apart from tiring him out it is essential for the baby to be talked to, smiled at and generally stimulated to ensure the best possible development of his brain and faculties. Right through childhood intellectual activity can be as tiring as physical exertion – very often the first time a child sleeps really well is after starting school.

FIRST FEW WEEKS

During the day try to keep the baby in a place where he can hear family life going on around him. Put him in a carry-cot or basket rather than in his cot, so that you can move him around easily, and while he is lying awake hang a brightly coloured mobile within view, or position him so that he can see out of the window. If you are lucky enough to have somewhere out of doors where he can lie in the pram then put it under the trees where he can watch the fascinating changing patterns of light and dark.

At night, although he may be awake and asleep in the same proportions as during the day, try to make the wakeful periods as unstimulating and boring as possible – don't chat to him or put the light on while changing and feeding.

'The amount of time that a baby is active during the day can affect the amount he will sleep later.'

22

GETTING BIGGER

As he begins to take in more of the world around him it becomes easier to make the difference between day and night more marked. There are some excellent pieces of equipment that can be indispensable in making his day as enjoyable and active as possible.

When he is about a month old it is worth investing in a bouncing cradle. The great advantage of one of these is that he can watch you and the rest of the family from a comfortable propped up position and that he can kick his legs and wave his arms freely which in turn will make the chair gently bounce. It is better than propping him up on cushions where however carefully you do it he will almost certainly have sunk into an undignified and uncomfortable heap a few minutes later. It's surprising how much movement can be achieved by persistent squirming and kicking. You can buy brightly coloured beads or jolly little men that fix onto the bouncing cradle and very soon he will try to reach forward and touch them. I found with Alexander that it made it more interesting for him if I varied the beads by covering one of them with shiny silver foil or different coloured paper – it was fascinating to see him try to touch the 'new' one. If you do this make sure the paper is securely fastened so there's no danger of the baby managing to get it off and put it in his mouth. Move the chair from time to time so that he can either see you or some other interesting view – the television can be the most wonderful source of light, colour and sound to stimulate a baby. It somehow makes me feel rather guilty to be switching on the television for a three month old baby, and I'm irrationally quite pleased when there's something on that could be termed educational. If television had been marketed as a 'baby-stimulator' I'm sure I wouldn't feel that way: there really couldn't be anything better for the purpose. As soon as he is able to grasp things give him a noisy, colourful rattle to wave about.

Of course not all babies will settle happily into sitting in a chair or lying awake in a cradle – there are some who only seem to be content while being carried around. For these I am sure it is right to give them what they want. Buy a sling or baby carrier and accept the fact that the housework or whatever will have to be done with your baby attached – in many other cultures this is the general rule, and it certainly gives the baby a wonderful sense of security and comfort. If his father or an older brother or sister can take a turn to give you a break then so much the better – it is surely preferable to hearing an unhappy baby lying in his cot crying. The only snag is that carrying him around will be very likely to make him drop off to sleep (see p. 48) so he may not have as much time active and awake during the day as you would wish. Try some loud chat as you move around, and every few days have another go at putting him into a bouncing cradle – the clinging phases often come and go, particularly if he is indulged in his need to be carried when necessary and not left to cry.

'However carefully you prop him up on cushions he will almost certainly sink into an undignified and uncomfortable heap.'

WATER

Playing in water is not only enormous fun but very tiring for babies and toddlers. Sometimes bathing the baby in the evening can help his sleep and can become part of a winding-down ritual which will be very important as he grows older. If Dad is out at work all day then this can be a very good time for him to take over the care of the baby and for them to enjoy each other's company. Start to introduce bath toys into the routine and make the whole procedure fun and exhausting.

As soon as possible take him swimming – there are now a number of swimming baths around the country which include specially warm pools for babies and toddlers. Don't take him if the water is cold: not only will the baby hate it but you will get very shivery yourself having to stand still so much of the time. Both of you will be miserable and it might put the baby off what should be an extremely enjoyable activity. Many places have classes for mothers and babies and these are well worth joining – apart from the fun and hopefully the good sleep that will follow it is very important that the baby should learn to swim as soon as possible for safety's sake. If you can take a friend with you the first few times then so much the better. You'll want to get the baby dried and dressed as quickly as possible after swimming and it can be a bit miserable trying to handle a slippery wet little creature on a shallow wooden bench while standing shivering in your own soaking swimsuit.

EXERCISE

Usually at about six months, or earlier if he can support his head with complete confidence, the baby can start using a baby bouncer. This is a sling seat made from material hung on a strong piece of elastic with the baby's feet just touching the floor, so that when he kicks he bounces up and down vigorously. It is suspended either from a frame of its own or from a hook in the ceiling – if you are using one of the carrycot hammocks (p. 34) then one or two strategically placed hooks can be used for both.

'Playing in water is not only enormous fun but very tiring.'

These bouncers have very good 'tiredness value' and are great fun. Katie would be happy in one for about ten minutes — very good going for her — and it's amazing how much you can accomplish in that time if you're the parent of a restless baby. The rarity of having two free hands makes you really appreciate it when you do, and zoom around getting six things done at once.

Once he starts pulling himself up on things and showing signs of trying to stand then one of the baby walkers on wheels is a very good way of encouraging him and using up energy.

As a general rule bring out toys, rattles, books and so on in rotation rather than always the same selection every day, to produce as much variety as possible and avoid boredom. There are now toy libraries that you can join. It's always the forbidden things like handbags, keys, china ornaments, glasses and so on that prove irresistible to nosey fingers, so try to keep surprising him with similarly exciting new 'toys' of his own. Alexander for instance had his own set of keys made up of lots of old unused ones put into an old handbag which he would play with for hours.

Going out in the fresh air from as young an age as possible nearly always improves a baby's sleeping. Taking the pram out to do the shopping or for a walk in the park, then later on the buggy or pushchair not only makes the baby's day more interesting but will certainly help to tire him out. Some supermarkets now have trolleys with a special raised section in which you can lie a baby, and many of them have assistants who will help you to pack up and load the shopping — my babies always seem to get hungry just as I reach the queue at the till and have to be taken out and carried to prevent uproar. I have breast fed in the most extraordinary places, but I think a supermarket checkout would be going a bit far. I did have to stop on the way back from the village shop on a country walk once and feed by the side of the road: it felt rather like something out of Thomas Hardy.

Try to find a local mother and toddler group and use the excellent one o'clock clubs.

ENVIRONMENT

WHERE TO SLEEP

One of the first and most important decisions to be made is where the baby is going to sleep. In many other cultures the baby automatically sleeps with its parents, often in the same bed and sometimes until the age of six or seven. This avoids naturally many of the so-called sleep problems that we in the West suffer from: we expect a great deal of a new born baby when we banish him to a separate, silent room all on his own after he has spent nine months in the warmth and security of his mother's womb. Many British families are now bringing their children into the same bedroom and even into the family bed, but this may not always be the perfect solution.

In the early stages if you are breastfeeding then there is no doubt that it is infinitely more restful for both mother and baby to have him next to you in bed. Neither of you has to wake fully when the baby is hungry – you can just roll over and feed him as you doze, and as he will hardly need to cry to alert you then there is more chance of the rest of the family being undisturbed. It's a lovely feeling to have a warm snuggly baby next to you in bed to cuddle. The worry that many people have about lying on top of their babies and suffocating them is a false one – unless one of the parents is drunk or drugged research has shown that even in deep sleep they will be aware of the baby and move away from him when necessary. I do think though that it is worth pushing the bed against a wall and having the baby between you and the wall and when you feed the other side between you and your husband, so that you are confident he will not fall out – otherwise you may spend much of the night tense and half aware of keeping him safe, which means you won't get much relaxed sleep. If you can't put the bed against the wall then push a large piece of furniture against it, or two heavy chairs. And if you're a single parent or your husband is away then obviously you will have to take these precautions on the other side as well.

There are of course some disadvantages to having the baby in bed with you. Theoretically he should space out his feeds naturally so that after a few months he is only waking once or twice in the night, but I found with Alexander this didn't really happen. He slept in bed with us from birth, as I found it much more trouble to keep getting in and out of bed to feed him, and also of course it had the enormous advantage that instead of the sometimes impossible business of getting him back to sleep after a feed by rocking, singing, patting and so on, he would just drift off peacefully next to me, with no effort on my part at all. For the first few months it worked very well, and I got much more sleep than I had with Katie who had slept in a cradle.

Alexander was a large baby who needed to feed very often but as he got bigger he did indeed start to sleep longer between feeds. Then however he started gradually to return to the frequent feeds, and eventually couldn't sleep at all unless constantly at the breast. This I began to find very tiring and when I did decide to move him to his own bed it was a long and difficult process.

Film taken over a few nights of a baby sleeping next to its mother has shown that the baby rarely goes for longer than twenty minutes or so between feeds, certainly when newborn, and I have no doubt that having the baby next to you is the natural way and that the frequent small feeds are as nature intended but in our society where one is expected to keep going for most of the day then obviously a certain amount of uninterrupted sleep at night is essential. As with so many aspects of baby care the success of sharing the bed depends on the temperaments of both mother, father and baby and must remain an individual decision. With Rory I took a midway course and had him in bed for the first few weeks then transferred him to a cradle once he was in the habit of going straight back to sleep after feeds. At the time of writing this has so far worked pretty well. He does still wake for night feeds, but at least he goes back to sleep in between and the gaps are definitely getting longer.

Apart from the possible difficulty of getting the baby out of the family bed and into his own another problem of bed sharing can be the reaction of other members of the family. Many husbands would be very unhappy at the idea of a third member of the family in the marital bed and if it is going to cause any friction then it is obviously not worth it. If your husband is uncertain but not definitely against it then it may be worth a try — he will probably get more sleep with the baby in the bed being fed on the instant he wakes than he would being woken by screams from a cradle across the room or next door.

There is the common worry that a couple's sex life will suffer, but in practice this is rarely a problem — a deeply sleeping baby is pretty oblivious to everything going on around him, and in the words of the song 'love will find a way'! However there will undoubtedly be many husbands who will resent the intrusion of the baby into bed, and for these families another arrangement must be made. I'm lucky enough to have a partner who will go along with anything that will help me to get more sleep — I can be so unbearably irritable and short tempered after a particularly bad night that all the family has learnt how important it is that Mum gets some rest.

Another reaction to be taken into account is the jealousy of the siblings. It may be hard enough to take the arrival of a new baby without discovering him in the parents' bed and some tactful transferring early in the morning may be necessary to avoid discovery. Alternatively be prepared for an invasion by the other child or children and to eventually all sleeping together in a true 'family bed'.

If you do decide to have one or all of them in with you then you will need an extra large bed so that you can all sleep reasonably well. As these are extremely expensive to buy a better solution is either to construct a simple wooden platform on which you put two mattresses crosswise or else to push a couple of beds together, again placing the mattresses across them. Even if the children don't sleep with you all the time it is

'The beautiful cradles you see in the big stores are very tempting.'

wonderful to have a large comfortable space for them to snuggle into when ill, or even for cosy Sunday mornings all together. The main point to remember is that there is absolutely nothing wrong with bringing children into your bed if it feels natural to you, and that no one should let comments by neighbours or relatives put them off. Some parents have their first good night's sleep for years after bringing the normally sleepless child into their bed. I am sure that many babies and young children are very lonely in rooms on their own, and this may well be a factor in their waking at night.

If you decide not to have baby in the same bed then the next decision is where to put him. If you are feeding on demand then you will certainly be up several times in the night at first, and it's much easier to have him in the same room. Right next to your bed can be a very good place as you can reach him quickly and probably without getting out of bed. The only snag is that if you are basically lazy like I am then you may find you don't put him back after feeding – it's so easy to snuggle down and drop off together rather than make the effort to tuck him back into his cot and maybe have to do some rocking, patting and singing before you can creep back into your own bed. If this happens several times then you're back to square one and he's sleeping in your bed. I have had to put the crib over the other side of the bedroom so that I am forced to get out of bed each time he wakes – by the time I reach him I am just about fully awake and strong minded enough not to take him back into bed. If he's the sort of baby that does need some walking or rocking after a feed to get back to sleep then this is a way Dad can share in the nights even if you are breast feeding.

If he's a very noisy sleeper or you have a tiny bedroom then you may not want to share it with him. In this case an adjoining room is the best. Even if you can hear him via a baby alarm, padding along corridors or up and down stairs in the middle of the night is not much fun, and the sooner you reach him the less worked up he will be and the more likely to have a calm feed and go off to sleep again. He must be somewhere you are confident that you will hear him without having to strain, or you will never relax enough to go deeply to sleep. If you are a very light sleeper or he is a noisy sleeper then a room next door can even be preferable to being in your room, otherwise you will wake at all his little snuffles and gurgles when he is not really ready for a feed.

Make the room as light, bright and cheerful as possible, and put up some interesting pictures and mobiles. Later on when he begins to understand that it is his own bedroom it will be very important that you have made it somewhere he enjoys being.

If you are not sure that you will easily hear him then fix up a baby alarm so that you can sleep without worrying. Some of them have a talk-back switch so that you can comfort the baby by the sound of your voice, but the only time I ever tried to use one Katie nearly leapt out of the cot with the shock. I suppose your mother's voice suddenly booming out from a little box must seem a bit strange.

AND IN WHAT

When you have decided on the position then you must choose what he is going to sleep in. The beautiful cradles you see in the big stores draped in ribbon and lace are very tempting but quite unnecessary and very expensive. As long as he is warm, securely wrapped and lying on something reasonably soft then a baby can sleep in just about anything. It's best to have something quite small at first as a full size cot can give him too much overwhelming space and it can be difficult to make him feel cosy and secure. As he will probably have been in a hospital crib for a few days something of a similar size is probably suitable. The old fashioned idea of using a drawer or box is perhaps a little too practical – it's not every day a new baby comes home and it's enjoyable for everybody to put the baby into something reasonably attractive. A wicker baby basket is not too expensive, is easy to move around and looks very pretty. Make sure it is lined all round the sides or else buy or make a lining to fit it to prevent draughts. Alternatively if you are going to be travelling later on with the baby then a carrycot is the answer as it can be safely strapped onto the back seat of the car and is easy to move around.

The carrycot or basket should be put on a sofa, low table or two chairs pushed together as the floor would be too draughty and very uncomfortable for you to reach. If you already have the cot that the baby will be moved into later then the carrycot can be placed inside it.

If you can afford it then of course it is ideal to have a proper cradle. It is rather an extravagance as he will not be in it for more than a few months, but a cradle can look very attractive and if you buy a rocking one can be very helpful in getting the baby to sleep. Up until this century most cradles were made with rockers and I can't understand why this practice didn't continue − all babies are soothed by movement and it's much less tiring just to reach out an arm and rock the cradle than to take the baby out and walk round the room or rock him in your arms. There are now one or two rocking cradles available and it may be worth investing in one straight away.

Most cradles of course rock or swing from side to side: an even more soothing movement is that of up and down − nearer to the motion experienced while inside the mother.

In 1969 a London doctor discovered that babies stop crying if rocked up and down at a critical speed of 60−70 times a minute. A recent invention has made it possible to achieve this very simply. Mr and Mrs Owens were desperate with their crying baby until they discovered that she could be calmed by their holding the carrycot between them and lifting it up and down. Howard Owens set about making a net to hold a carrycot suspended by a strong spring from a hook in the ceiling − it worked so well that he started to manufacture them and sell them by mail order from his home. I only wish I'd had one for Katie and Alexander: Rory is relatively so easy going that it's hard to tell how effective it is for him, but there are many satisfied parents to testify to its success, and the Owens even give a 'peace or money back' guarantee.

Vertical rocking is nothing new − in parts of Africa they suspend their babies in hammocks to achieve a very similar effect. In America they now make cradles that stand on a spring at each corner that will rock up and down at a push. I should have thought it would be possible for a handyman to construct a similar one at home. A wooden box with a spring at each corner in which you place the carrycot should be very effective.

For daytime sleeps put the carrycot anywhere that is conveniently within earshot. If the weather is mild and you are lucky enough to have somewhere available then he could spend some time out of doors. Make sure that the carrycot or pram is covered with a net to prevent any possible danger from cats.

As soon as you feel the baby is finding it uncomfortable in his cradle or carrycot or is trying to sit up, usually at 4–6 months, then move him to a full sized cot. A traditional drop-sided one is best, and make sure it conforms to the required safety standards, particularly as regards the distance between the bars, which should be no more than about 7cm apart.

'Little stone-age babies must have lain on some very interesting furs.'

BEDDING

Whichever type of cradle you choose the bedding is very important and can be a factor in encouraging peaceful sleep. Make sure you buy one of the modern mattresses with ventilation holes at one end so that there is no danger of suffocation. Cover this with an elasticated bottom sheet which will stay smooth and unwrinkled. If you suspect that your baby may be waking because he is cold you could try one of the thermal pads underneath him – however warm you make the room it is not the same as lying on something which is warm in itself which of course is how it would be if the baby was lying on his mother. There are special electric pads available such as they use in hospitals but I find the thought of electricity in a baby's bed rather alarming, especially as there is a possibility of his being wet in the night. You could use one to warm up the cot and then turn it off when you put him to bed, but a hot water bottle removed at the last minute would do the job just as well.

Alternatively you can replace the undersheet with one of the lambskins which have become very popular recently. These are claimed to keep the baby warm in winter and cool in summer and many people swear that the baby sleeps much better and also seems happier lying on one while awake during the day. The theory is that the wool caresses the baby as he moves around. There is no danger of suffocation as air can circulate freely through the strands of wool. Research has shown that babies do seem to feel very secure and comfortable on one of these and in premature baby units it was found that babies kept on lambskins actually gained weight faster than those on ordinary sheets. Certainly one great asset is that if the baby does seem very happy on a skin then you can lie him on it during the day and take it with you travelling and he will have a constant source of security. In one hospital they tried making artificial lambskins and they didn't have the same effect – the babies sucked at the man-made fibres and tried to eat them and didn't seem happy at all.

I have tried one for the purposes of the book and Rory

certainly seems very happy on it – he sort of snuggles into it as he settles down, and he drifts off to sleep more easily than he did on a sheet. It's difficult to know if he feels cool in summer and warm in winter; I've tried asking him but at three months he just won't give me a straight answer. I shall have to write an appendix to the book when he's old enough to tell me.

Again this is nothing new – the use of animals skins on which to nurse babies has been common practice in many parts of the world including our own for hundreds of years. Little stone-age babies must have lain on some very interesting furs. It is extraordinary how in so many ways we are coming full circle; having been through the modern ideas of bottle feeding, separate cots, technological childbirth and so on our society seems to be gradually reverting to a simpler, more natural way of looking after our babies. Rory looks quite mediaeval on his lambskin in his wooden rocking cradle. If we can only combine the best of both worlds and use our wonderful modern technology in a gentler less regimented more loving way then we should be able to produce some very healthy, happy children.

Whether you have an undersheet or a lambskin you will of course need to cover the baby with something for most of the year; here again there are many choices. In most cases it's best to have a cotton or polyester sheet between baby and blanket as wool can be rather itchy and uncomfortable and in a few may even cause an allergic reaction. The sheet can be tucked into the mattress very tightly thus making the baby feel secure and having an effect like swaddling (p. 45) or you can swaddle him properly by wrapping the sheet right round him and he won't need another one over him. You can either buy little cot sheets or cut up some old full sized ones of your own. Then a light but warm woollen blanket or two depending on the temperature of the room – some of the man-made fibre ones are very good but probably not quite as warm. Finish with a pretty cover if you like – perhaps when the grandparents come to visit.

Alternatively a duvet can replace sheet and blankets and is very light as well as warm. Although they are not really meant to be tucked in, if you feel the baby likes it as so many do then you can always turn the duvet sideways and tuck it firmly under the mattress.

Never give a baby a pillow – it is quite unnecessary and can even carry a slight risk of suffocation. You can now buy ones made with ventilation holes like the mattress which are an improvement, but I still see no point in having one – it may look more comfortable to us because we are so used to sleeping with pillows, but to a baby it is more natural and healthier for the back and shoulders to sleep without one.

Don't overload the baby with bedding – lightness with warmth is the key. Recent research has shown that if anything we tend to overheat our babies – it's less dangerous to be slightly

'It is a good idea to change into something different at bedtime.'

too cold than to be too hot. When he moves into a full sized cot the alternatives in bedding are very similar. A duvet is probably the simplest and most comfortable choice.

NIGHTWEAR

For dressing the baby himself it's obviously not essential to have pyjamas or a nightdress in the early stages but it is a good idea to change into something different at bedtime as it all helps to underline the difference between day and night. If not pyjamas then a comfortable Babygro over a vest is quite adequate, but if he proves later to be the type to fling off all his bedclothes you may need to buy one of the warmer all in one sleep suits with feet. If you do buy pyjamas for an older baby make sure the top is long enough to tuck well into the trousers or that it has elastic loops and buttons to keep the two halves together – there's nothing more miserable than a cold midriff in the middle of the night. If he is a very active baby you can try to guard against later problems of his climbing out of his cot in the middle of the night by putting him now into a cosy baby-bag. If he has always worn one at night then he will not object to being in one later on and it will make climbing almost impossible.

Don't be tempted to overdress him – as with bedding and room temperature we often tend to overheat our babies. In the summer on a very warm night then a vest and nappy will be enough or even just a nappy in really hot weather.

If you find it difficult to change his nappy in the middle of the night without waking him up completely then slip a disposable nappy pad inside his usual one. This will absorb considerably more wetness and probably keep him comfortable right through the night; it may look bulky but he almost certainly won't mind. A one way liner also helps to keep his skin dry and prevent nappy rash. Babies seem to vary considerably as to whether they mind being in a wet nappy or not – if yours does then he must of course be changed as soon as he's uncomfortable but have everything ready nearby for as many changes as you think he may need and do them as quickly and quietly as possible without

39

putting the light on. If it's just wet you may be able to change him with one hand while feeding him; I could sometimes manage it. It feels rather satisfying to be dealing with both ends at once. If you can afford them then disposable nappies are wonderfully quick and easy and the new elasticated ones are far more leakproof than they used to be: it also means no depressing bucket of soaking nappies for you to deal with in the morning.

In our climate he will nearly always need a vest − I have always used the type that do up between the legs with poppers. They seem more cosy than the short type, help to keep the nappy in position and prevent riding up and a cold gap in the middle of the night.

LIGHT AND DARK

The amount of light in the room will not affect a new born baby one way or the other but it is a good idea to have it fairly dark to help him recognise night-time. Don't have it pitch black as it will be difficult to feed and change him without having to put on a light. A door slightly ajar with a light left on outside is preferable to buying a special night light which he may get so used to that it will be difficult for him to sleep without it later on. You can buy a low wattage bulb to make it less expensive. There seems to be an instinctive fear of complete darkness that appears in many young children whether they have been brought up with or without a light and I am against trying to make them 'brave it out'. This may appear to work but it may be that they are only bottling up their fear to please you and it may manifest itself in some other way. It seems to me unnecessarily cruel.

TEMPERATURE

The room need not be excessively warm. Many hospital nurseries are kept at a high temperature as some of the smaller babies may tend to be cold but there is no need to keep the baby's room at the same level once you get home. Don't judge it entirely by the way you feel however, as babies spend much of their time immobile and so will generate less heat than you do. Just make sure the room is comfortably warm and that the air doesn't feel cold to breathe, especially for a new born baby or one that is unwell. It may be cheaper to buy a separate heater for the baby's room, rather than have to step up the heating for the whole of the house. If you're ever worried as to whether the baby is too hot or cold then gently feel the back of his neck: it should feel nicely warm. Cold hands or feet are not necessarily an indication that he is too cold altogether.

NOISE

As with light and dark a newborn baby's sleep will be relatively unaffected by noise. Many people recommend that he should sleep surrounded by a certain amount of sound so that he will become used to it and be able to sleep more easily later on and without having to have complete silence. I'm not sure that this really works – my sister and I were brought up identically and yet she always has to have complete dark and silence to sleep well whereas I am happier with some light and can sleep through a certain amount of noise (except that of a baby crying!) It seems sensible to me to let his daytime naps be surrounded by family hustle and bustle but to reinforce the change to night-time by keeping his bedroom reasonably quiet. There are some sounds of course that are very soothing to a sleeping baby, and I mention some of these on page 53.

GETTING TO SLEEP

Many of the baby care books of twenty years ago or so recommended that the baby should be left in his cot to cry himself to sleep, and that if you went to him or even worse picked him up you were 'spoiling' him and setting a pattern that would never change. The experts nowadays, I am glad to say, nearly all agree that it is not possible to spoil a tiny baby, and that far from teaching him bad habits by going to him when he needs you, you are equipping him with a sense of security and love which will last him all his life and make him all the more capable of giving love himself. There is of course a sort of settling down to sleep grizzling which a parent knows is not serious and will quickly stop and it's certainly not a good idea to rush to the baby at the slightest sound, but any genuine distress I believe should be attended to. In many other cultures it is extremely rare to hear a baby cry, and it is odd that in our society we should have come to accept such an upsetting sound as part of everday life. Certainly we seem to have been designed to respond quickly to it — there are very few commonly heard sounds at the same high frequency, and yet our hearing is particularly acute at that range. There may come a time when the baby is older when you have to let him complain for bursts of five minutes or so (see p. 76), but in the early stages the more you go to him when he needs you the more independent he will be as a child.

Obviously it will not hurt the baby to be left occasionally for a few minutes to cry a little as you certainly don't want to feel you have to let your entire life be dominated by his demands, but as a general rule tiny babies cry because they need something or are

'There's no law against pushing a pram out at 2.00 in the morning.'

unhappy. There can't be any hard and fast rules about such things and finally it must remain an individual decision – many parents do leave their babies to cry and they grow up without any apparent ill effects, but I just find it impossible to listen to a young baby crying for any length of time without going to him.

A new born baby will sleep whenever he needs to without any extra encouragement, usually straight after a feed, and will probably only wake again when he is hungry. My three babies all followed the same pattern of sleeping for four to five hours at a stretch for the twenty-four hours after delivery and then changing to almost constant feeds for the next couple of days.

Apart from making sure he is warm and comfortable for these first few days you can leave it entirely to your baby to drop off naturally at any time of day or night. After a few days however you may find that he needs a little help to get peacefully off to sleep – if you are sure he's not hungry or in pain but doesn't seem to settle in the cot then your natural instinct will be to pick him up and cuddle him which of course is exactly the right thing to do. After all he's been used to complete security, warmth and the soothing sounds and movement of your body for nine months, and to expect him to feel at home all on his own in a cradle may be asking too much of him. The ideal solution for the first few nights is to take him into your bed where he will fall asleep happily at your side after a feed. (See p. 28 for more about bringing him into your bed). This may not suit you for any length of time, and in any case the baby will be sleeping much of the daytime to start with and for these sleeps may need to be helped to drop off on his own.

Also after the first few days it's a good idea to encourage him to fall asleep without always having to be on the breast or sucking from a bottle or later on you may find he has great difficulty getting to sleep without one of them, and may continue waking in the night for 'comfort feeds' when he's not really hungry. This can be a difficult habit to break.

POSITION

When you put him down in his bed you will have to decide for him whether he will sleep on his front or on his back. It will probably become clear quite quickly which he likes – usually on the front seems to be preferred. Research has shown that babies lying on their stomachs sleep longer than those on their backs, and of course if they should bring up small amounts of milk there is less danger of their choking. I like to vary the head position from side to side, and in any case by three months or so the baby will be able to turn it himself.

SWADDLING

One of the oldest ways of helping a baby to settle calmly into sleep is to swaddle him. The custom of swaddling is a very ancient one and until the eighteenth century was used in almost all societies. The baby was wrapped very tightly in bands of cloth so that the legs were kept together and the arms held by the sides. Then the baby was often strapped to a cradle board which could be propped up or hung within sight and sound of the mother. We tend to think of this use of tight bands and cradle boards as cruel and inhibiting, but studies of cultures where it is still practised such as the Navajo Indians show that the babies are not kept this way all the time and that it undoubtedly calms and soothes them into sleep or into a quiet alert state. Used sensibly it does not hamper physical progress at all. Perhaps because they spend less time crying and more time calmly aware of their surroundings, if anything swaddled babies advance more quickly than unswaddled ones.

In our culture in recent years a form of semi-swaddling has returned – in hospitals babies are frequently wrapped tightly in a cotton sheet before being tucked into their cots, and it's certainly worth pursuing this at home. A light woollen shawl or cellular baby blanket may be more effective than cotton, and as wool is slightly stretchy you are less likely to wrap him too tightly. Lie the baby on the shawl and gently wrap it around him, tucking the ends under his body to hold it in place.

For a new-born baby the arms are best wrapped by his sides, but later on if he still enjoys swaddling bend his arms at the elbow and try to leave his forearms free so that he can suck at his fingers if he likes.

'I would have given Katie fifty bright green dummies.'

SUCKING

Some babies suck their fingers or thumbs at a very early age –
there are even some who start in the womb – and as long as it is
not a constant habit it doesn't necessarily mean that he isn't
being allowed long enough at the breast or bottle, and it can be a
very comforting way for a baby to soothe himself to sleep. As
long as you are sure that you are feeding him enough and that he
is allowed to suck at the breast long enough to keep up your milk
supply (see p. 14), then there is no reason why you shouldn't
gently encourage his thumb into his mouth if he seems to want
to go on sucking – it's certainly less tiring than having him
constantly at the breast which of course is really what he's after.
Certainly of those babies that are not always allowed to fall

asleep at the breast then research shows that those who suck their thumbs or use a dummy on the whole have less problems in getting to sleep than those who don't. Some people are strongly against the use of dummies but I found one invaluable for soothing my colicky daughter. The disadvantages are that they can easily get lost, that they may get dirty and that they look rather unattractive but these are unlikely to deter anyone who is really desperate to help a fretful, sleepless baby.

It's amazing how many preconceived ideas have to be abandoned once you have a baby. I had all sorts of theories about the upbringing of children which very quickly bit the dust once I had real live ones of my own — much against my original principles I would have given Katie fifty bright green dummies if it would have got her to sleep. There are times such as when I find myself on Alexander's orders being a tipper truck at 6.30 in the morning when I wonder if I've gone over a little too far to the enemy.

If used sensibly and not stuck in whenever the baby cries in place of food or cuddles, there's no doubt a dummy can be very helpful in getting the baby to sleep, never of course, dipped in or filled with anything sweet. Sometimes he will wake again as soon as it falls out of his mouth which can be quite a problem. If his cradle is next to your bed and you have a supply of clean dummies readily to hand so that you don't have to grope around in the dark looking for the lost one then this needn't be insurmountable. I don't like the idea of pinning or tying one onto the nightclothes as however short the ribbon there is always the fear that it might catch around his neck or even just tangle uncomfortably in his fingers.

Apart from swaddling and sucking the magic words to remember in getting a baby to sleep are rhythm, movement and sound, preferably all combined at the same time. None of these will work or course if the baby is hungry or uncomfortable but once you are sure he has fed enough and is not wet, messy or in pain then the following methods are worth trying.

RHYTHM AND MOVEMENT

One of the most natural ways of getting a baby to sleep is by rocking. It has been proved in experiments that gentle rocking at a rate of 60–90 rocks a minute will calm most babies. This corresponds of course to the heartbeat that the baby heard in the womb, and there is a natural instinct in most parents to pick up a crying baby and walk him around at a rate that will gently jog him up and down at just about that magic speed. Try putting him over your left shoulder – sometimes known as the parrot position – and pacing up and down. The left shoulder is said to be best because the baby can feel your heartbeat against him but I suspect that it feels more natural for most of us as it leaves the right hand free.

If your baby brings up as much milk as my three then you'll soon get used to all your clothes having rather unpleasant sticky marks on the left shoulders. I've never been efficient enough to always drape myself with a clean muslin square before carrying them. I find in any case that it's hopeless trying to look smart when bringing up young children – if it isn't sick on the shoulder then it's play dough or paint all down my front.

If walking alone doesn't seem to help then try patting him quite hard on the back or bottom, as rhythmically as possible. Then try bouncing up and down while walking – rather uncomfortable but often effective. Sometimes going up and down stairs while holding the baby can achieve the same result – my sister and brother-in-law must have worn holes in their stair carpet while persuading their insomniac daughter to drop off to sleep.

A less tiring way of achieving the rate of 60 rocks a minute in an up and down movement is by using a Lullababy hammock (p. 34). These are extremely successful in soothing babies to sleep and will save your time, energy and temper. If you have several hooks in the house then you can pop the baby into one and carry on with getting the supper, getting the other children to bed or just putting your feet up for a moment.

A baby sling or carrier is another good way of giving the baby the warmth, security and movement he may be needing while leaving your arms free. There are various different types to buy, or you can make a sling out of a shawl or baby sheet, but I've never managed that very successfully. I found the sort that do up with a simple clip at the back, with the baby positioned comfortably on my chest the most effective. A carrier is extremely useful during the day for carrying the baby while shopping, cleaning and so on and as they often send the baby to sleep then they can also be used in the evening or night-time in the house for a baby that needs lengthy walking to get him to sleep. I found that the baby had to be completely full up before putting him in the sling, as otherwise being so close to the food supply would remind him of that little bit of room he had left and he wouldn't be able to settle. Even when fully fed I found that the baby would sometimes protest for a few minutes when first put in but as long as I kept walking briskly round the room and even if necessary up and down the stairs or out of the front door and back again then he would soon go to sleep. Yes I did get a few strange looks as I marched out onto the doorstep, danced around a bit in the fresh air then disappeared back into the house again, but at the time that was the least of my problems. You may feel exhausted after having the baby in one for any length of time at first but it's surprising how quickly your shoulders get used to the weight, and after a while you can more or less carry on with your evening routine as normal.

It's amazing how babies who like to be carried can sense the minute you sit down — even if you try to keep up the same rocking, jogging motion with your upper half they seem to receive signals directly from your legs informing them the moment you should attempt anything as outrageous as trying to have a minute's rest. Occasionally a rocking chair can fool a baby like this — another old-fashioned but effective piece of equipment. Rocking gently to and fro with the baby on your shoulder, a drink in your hand and a good book to read or television programme to watch can be a very relaxing way of getting the baby to sleep. If he cries every time you put him down then don't keep trying to force it, it will only end with both of you being frustrated and tired. Just let him sleep wherever he's comfortable — there will eventually come a moment later in the evening when you can sense that he's really deeply asleep enough to move.

Some babies can be rocked to sleep in their own cradle which of course is much easier. After having gone out of fashion for many years there are now a few reasonably priced ones you can buy, and it's certainly worth trying one if your baby seems to like this sort of motion.

I didn't have one for Katie or Alexander but while writing this book I have been trying Rory in a wooden swinging cradle during the day and it does seem to send him off to sleep beautifully. My sister-in-law in Los Angeles has a carrycot suspended in a frame which can be wound up and then swings for 45 minutes. It always gets her baby Victoria Jane to sleep. I haven't seen the same over here, but there is a swing seat which is set in a very similar frame which also winds up. It's really meant for sitting in and swinging for fun of course, but a friend of mine had a baby who could only be got to sleep in one of these: it was a bit tricky getting her out without waking her but if she waited until the baby was deeply asleep then she could just manage it. I've tried one at home and it does always send Rory to sleep, and also seems to keep him happier when he's feeling a bit colicky in the evenings. I imagine pretty soon they will sell a carrycot that swings but until then the swing seat, although expensive, would be worth buying if you're really desperate. Perhaps a clever handyman could adapt the seat to make it easier to remove the sleeping baby.

Patting the baby on the back or side is another good thing to try — my own babies have all responded well to being patted firmly on the back in their cots while lying on their fronts. Katie seemed to need a sort of gentle shaking from a hand held firmly on her back, while Rory goes to sleep with a rythmic patting on the bottom from one hand with the other one held firmly on his back. I even try to mimic the rhythm of a heartbeat with the bottom-patting hand: a sort of double beat every second or so. If that doesn't work then lifting the whole basket up and down in a

'The magic words in getting baby to sleep are rhythm, movement and sound.'

rocking movement while still patting his bottom with the other hand will sometimes do it.

One mother told me that she was taught by an amah in Hong Kong an ancient trick; you hold the baby on his side on your lap and gently pat his thigh with your hand, keeping up a steady rhythm. She said that it worked wonders for her children and for those of her friends as well.

I have read several articles lately on 'massaging' your baby – I can't honestly see that you need to learn any particular techniques, but of course the more physical contact you have with your baby the better, and a gentle rub with baby oil may well help to relax him and make him ready for sleep. Besides, it feels so lovely for both of you.

Some babies are sent off by the regular motion of a car and many a parent has driven round the streets in the middle of the night until his little Stirling Moss finally succumbed. It's a very useful technique for daytime naps too, and for many years we have had to plan our trips in the car around children's sleep times – if you have to drive somewhere too late in the day then of course they are bound to drop off and that means a bad night to follow. It generally works better with older babies and toddlers, but sometimes even tiny babies will respond. Strap the carrycot safely in the car and get your husband or a friend to drive so that you can sit in the back with the baby. Otherwise it can be very distracting for you to have the baby crying in the back and could be dangerous if you were tempted to keep turning round to see if he was all right. Older babies must of course be strapped safely in child-seats in the back. There are now some new models that recline into sleeping positions.

Walking him out in the pram in the fresh air is another good way of sending him off; the movement and change of atmosphere combined often settle a baby quickly, and there's no law that says you can't push a pram out at 2.0 in the morning if necessary unless it's too cold. You may get some strange looks from passers by but if you're finally getting the baby to sleep then you won't care one little bit how peculiar you look – children can drive one to do the most extraordinary things that

52

soon become part of everyday life and it's not until you look back that you realise just how odd some of your habits had become. For months I had to push Alexander round and round the block in his pram at lunchtime to get him off to sleep singing 'Pop Goes the Weasel' in a very loud monotonous voice and I used to get some very puzzled looks from the workmen on the scaffolding round the corner as I veered into view for the fourth and fifth time looking more and more desperate. Occasionally I would pass what was obviously a parent who understood and I would feel their sympathic and knowing glance.

If the pram pushing works in the evening then it's probably best not to transfer him but to leave him to sleep in the pram all night — some models have a top section which unclips from the wheels like a carrycot and can be carried into the bedroom. Or you can buy a set of wheels into which an ordinary carrycot will fit. You may not even need to wheel him outside; sometimes just a push around the room will do, and if you live in a flat then you can keep his carrycot permanently on the wheels and give him a little push around every time he threatens to wake.

SOUND

Singing to a baby is another very old method of soothing him — with all the rocking and patting ideas that I've mentioned it's worth trying some singing in his ear at the same time. Again rhythm and monotony are the key — lullabies are usually in a gently swinging sort of rhythm and the tunes also sound as if they rock up and down. Even if you feel you haven't the world's best singing voice it will sound wonderful to your baby — he'd rather have his Mum or Dad gently singing him to sleep than the greatest soprano in the world. There is also interesting recent research which shows that singing to a baby seems to be even more effective than just talking to him in terms of bringing on his ability to speak and become articulate. Mind you, as he grows older he may not appreciate your musical talents. I spent a good ten minutes the other night singing soothingly to a stony-faced Alexander, who finally looked me straight in the eye and said

'As he grows older he may not appreciate your musical talents ...'

'Yuk' very loudly and definitely. It didn't do much for any secret hopes I may have had of a singing career.

Some babies respond well to certain types of classical music, and it could be worth experimenting with some cassettes to see which particular composer your little one seems to favour.

Musical boxes are also well worth trying – sometimes if you start using one above his cot every time you put him to bed the baby will learn to associate the sound with going to sleep, and will drop off each night before the winding up runs out. You can buy mobiles which incorporate a musical box that hangs over the cot and provide him with visual and aural stimulation at the same time. Do make sure the mechanism keeps going for quite a long time before needing re-winding – it can be very frustrating if the music runs out just as the eyelids are getting heavy. A battery run model could be better.

There are other sounds apart from music which can sometimes have a magic effect – regular, droning sounds such as that of a vacuum cleaner, hairdryer or dishwasher for instance. It's obviously not a very satisfactory way of regularly getting him to sleep, as presumably his cot is not that close to the dishwasher, and you certainly don't want to let yourself in for vacuuming his bedroom every night until he drops off. But they can be useful emergency measures for a fretful baby, and if he does like that kind of noise then it will at least give you a free pair of hands when you do want to dry your hair or use something mechanical. You must never of course leave any electrical appliance switched on near a baby while you are out of the room.

A more sophisticated and scientifically based version of the droning sound is the recently developed 'womb music'. Recordings were made inside the mother's womb of the gurgles, swishing, rumblings and heartbeat that the baby would have heard while still inside, and it was found that playing these to crying babies would nearly always send them gently off to sleep. If started early enough these recordings really do seem to work. I have a little corner at the back of my mind that rather puritanically feels that it's somehow just putting off the fact that

'Some babies seem to respond well to certain types of classical music.'

the baby has got to learn to live in the outside world and that we shouldn't fool him that he's still in the womb, but that's quite illogical really. It's only an extension of all the rocking and singing techniques which are all to a certain extent mimicking life in the womb, and at any rate a desperate parent will quite rightly do anything to soothe a sleepless child. I was given a teddy bear with a cassette of womb music implanted in its tummy when Alexander was born – I did try to use it, but as he was so insatiably hungry for so much of his first few weeks I was never able to tell whether the womb music really helped or not, and by the time he was going for any reasonable length of time between feeds it was getting a bit late to start him on it. He does enjoy playing with it now – he carries it around switching on and off the 'funny noise'. Who knows, perhaps even at $2\frac{1}{4}$ he has a dim memory of life in the womb, and recognises unconsciously the soothing sounds.

You can now buy cassettes of womb music and classical music combined, which seems a very good idea.

ROUTINE

The older the baby gets the more important will routine become in ensuring peaceful bedtimes. After three or four months it's worthwhile trying to stick roughly to a regular bedtime and going through more or less the same ritual every night. This usually isn't something that has to be worked at – babies at around that age seem to slip into a fairly regular pattern of their own accord. The bedtime will probably be later at this stage than it will be as he gets older, but I think that's preferable to his being wide awake at four in the morning ready for fun and games. Whatever time he seems ready to settle down for the night then stick to it and go through more or less the same sequence of events. Set aside enough time to be able to bath and dress him without having to rush, if that is your particular evening routine, and to be able to go through whatever singing, rocking or patting ritual he seems to need. Put a cuddly toy or two in with him if you like – well away from his face of course. If he grows to associate them with comfort and going to sleep happily then it may make bedtime easier when he is older.

Try to accept the fact that he will take a specific amount of time to settle and allow plenty. If you are always aware of how late it's getting and how you're never going to get the supper cooked/children to bed/house tidied up if you don't start soon then the baby will probably sense it and take even longer to get to sleep. If you can put him down and leave him while still awake then so much the better, but don't put yourself through miseries about it at this stage — I couldn't with any of mine when they were very small. Later on as the baby gets older it will begin to matter much more or you may find yourself hanging around for ages each evening until your toddler drops off.

MEDICINES

On the whole I am completely opposed to the use of medicines to get a baby to sleep, but there may very occasionally come a time when the parents and baby are so desperate and have got themselves into such a state that a doctor may feel justified in prescribing a mild sedative for a few days, usually an antihistamine, to try to help the family as a whole. If it works then the baby will not only sleep better while on the course but hopefully his sleep pattern will have been permanently changed. It is not a satisfactory solution as apart from the distasteful idea of drugging a tiny baby occasionally the sedative can work the opposite way to that intended, and make the baby even more wakeful than usual. But it would be unrealistic to pretend that sedatives are not used by desperate parents — a surprisingly high percentage of babies are given them and it is reasonable not to close one's mind to the possibility that their use may be necessary. Hopefully you will find a more natural answer to your baby's sleeplessness even if it means waiting until he slips into a different pattern with time, and in any case never give any medicine without your doctor's advice.

'Herbs have been used for centuries to calm babies.'

Herbs on the other hand have been used for centuries to calm babies and help them sleep, and the majority of them are completely safe. Whether they work is not fully established, but the following is a selection of the herbs which are claimed to help.

Anise

Used to be known as 'Grandmother's gentle cure-all'. Completely harmless and the seeds made into a syrup are claimed to soothe babies.

Camomile

Camomile tea has been used as a calming, soporific drink for generations. They used to mix it with a little honey to administer it to babies.

Dill

'Dill procureth sleep,' so Galen said. The name comes from a Saxon word meaning to lull, and dill water has been used for this purpose for centuries.

Fennel

The Germans have used fennel to calm their babies for many years. Milupa now manufacture a drink made with fennel and glucose which may be safely given to babies.

Mint

In Jamaica they give their babies mint tea to help them sleep.

Alcohol

When I was at a particularly desperate pitch with Katie not sleeping someone recommended my giving her half a teaspoon of sherry — she was up all night wide awake and raring to go, obviously the type to be life and soul of the party in later years. Alcohol has been a traditional treatment for colicky or fretful babies for many years, but it's probably more useful for treating the parents in most cases. For babies I don't think it should be encouraged, but for people who may be shocked at the very idea it is interesting to note that the principal ingredient of gripe water, still sold over the counter as a cure for wind, is alcohol.

GETTING TO SLEEP SUMMARY CHART

Desperation Level	Have You Tried?	Page No.
One	Swaddling	45
	Thumb sucking	46
	Dummy	47
	Herbs	58
	Rocking cradle	48
	Singing	53
	Music	54
	Lambskin	36
Two	Rocking Chair	49
	Walking and rocking	49
	Going up and down stairs	49
	Droning	54
	Womb music	55
Three	Hammock	34
	Driving	52
	Walking Out	52
Four	Doctor	57
Five	Alcohol	59
Six	Mallet!	—

DISCOMFORT

There are many ways of course in which a baby can feel uncomfortable, and any one of them can be a factor in sleeplessness. You must try and eliminate all possible causes of irritation or pain before trying any of the ways of getting him to sleep, or your efforts will be wasted and you and the baby will end up very miserable.

WIND

We seem to have a bit of an obsession in this country about wind. In some parts of the world they have never heard of burping their babies or getting up their wind after feeds, and the babies don't appear to suffer any ill effects. But it does seem that many babies do feel discomfort if put down straight after a feed in a lying position, and in their case it's always best to get a good loud burp before attempting to get them to sleep. Methods vary in how to achieve this; with Alexander I found it easiest to hold him on my lap with one hand supporting his chest and chin while my other hand gently rubbed his back and sort of squeezed the air up and out. With Rory it seems to work best with him slung over my left shoulder and patted firmly on the back. There's nothing more satisfying than getting up a really good dose of wind but you must avoid the temptation to blame everything on to it. If a baby has been crying hard for some time then he will have been very likely to swallow some air, and the fact that he brings up some wind (or down from the other end) doesn't necessarily mean that it was the original cause of the trouble. Experience will tell with your baby as to whether he always needs to be burped after feeding, but if in doubt do it anyway — it's one less thing to worry about if he won't settle.

COLIC

Colic is a term used to cover a variety of problems which may or may not be connected with wind. Although some doctors would deny its existence I believe true colic does occur and is a very real physical condition. My first two babies undoubtedly had it — at an early evening feed they would suddenly stop after a few sucks, pull up their legs and scream violently and inconsolably. We suffered with them for a few days and then reluctantly gave them the anti-spasmodic drug that the doctor prescribed. It worked very well with both of them, although I found it difficult to give it to them the required 15 minutes before a feed, as babies fed on demand can be very unpredictable. Rory has been 'colicky' in the evenings but never badly enough to resort to using the drug. No doubt some would say that it was all due to tension in me and in the house in the evenings, and that with my third child I was more relaxed. I really don't think that was the cause although my anxiety may well have exacerbated the problem. Anyone who has had a baby with bad colic will be extremely tense and anxious by the time they get to the doctor and I think it can be very hard to be told that it may have all been caused by your tension and that you must relax or you will pass it on to the baby. Of course the baby senses your feelings but I believe in most cases the colic precedes the tension. Why it is so often early evening that seems to be the worst time is unexplained — in my case I wondered if it was because I had less milk towards the end of the day — which I definitely did — but as bottle fed babies also suffer evening colic that can't be the full explanation. In any case it seems very unsurprising that a tiny baby's intestines should take a few months to settle down as they don't have to start working until after the birth.

Whatever the cause, it can be a very miserable time for the whole family and any safe remedy is worth a try. Some breastfeeding mothers find that eliminating cows' milk in any

'Some medicines unfortunately taste really disgusting.'

form from their diet seems to help, suggesting that colic can be caused by an allergy to cows' milk protein. If you are going to try this then you must do it rigorously — there's no point in half measures as if the theory is correct then even the smallest trace of cows' milk in your diet will spoil the whole trial. Cut out butter, milk, cheese, yogurts and read the list of ingredients in everything you eat — for instance many biscuits contain whey powder. You can buy goats' milk and goats' milk products in many supermarkets now or try one of the new soya milks. Beware of the soft margarines — many of these contain milk products; I only found one spread which was completely safe: a kosher one called Tomor. Keep to this diet strictly for a week or two, and if you don't find any improvement then give it up. It didn't seem to help either of mine, but in my sister Clare's case it worked very well and some people report quite dramatic improvements. It's difficult to prove that it is really the mother's diet that is the cause as colic can come and go so suddenly in any case, and no mother is going to experiment with going off the diet just to prove a point.

Other foods eaten by the mother are often blamed for causing colic, and at one time or another I must have been told or read that almost everything edible can be guilty. Nuts, chocolate, grapes, cabbage, alcohol, spicy foods, plums, apples, etc. etc. There's no doubt that certain foods do seem to upset certain babies, and it's always worth cutting out something you are suspicious of to see if it helps – too much caffeine from drinking tea or coffee in large quantities goes straight through to the baby for instance. Also for a breastfeeding mother it is wise to eat regularly throughout the day and not save up for a large evening meal. For a bottle fed baby it is worth asking your doctor about changing the formula – perhaps onto a soya based one.

Sometimes a colicky baby seems to confuse his tummy pains with hunger, and he will try to feed to soothe himself – if it works then all well and good, a few extra feeds will not hurt, especially if he's breast fed. If, however, he gulps very fast and fills himself with air he may well make himself worse, and this is the time to try a dummy. Some people object to these but if it makes the baby feel better then it's worth it every time, even if you only use it for his colicky patches in the evening. If he is bottle fed then sometimes a smaller hole in the teat can help, by slowing down the speed at which he takes the milk. A friend of my sister's had very sore nipples and got hold of a National Childbirth Trust shield. She breast-fed very comfortably that evening and the baby seemed very contented. It wasn't for several hours that she discovered the shield had no hole in it – they leave you to make your own to the required size.

There are some wonderfully cheering pieces of research into

almost every aspect of child care: a good morale booster is that colicky babies are said to be more common in mothers of higher intelligence. The fact that I have had two with severe colic and a third without presumably confirms those depressing statistics about brain cells dying off as you get older – certainly when faced with Katie's maths homework I feel as if they've all given up the ghost already.

The important thing to remember about colic is that it will pass; perhaps not at the magic three month milestone so often quoted but certainly fairly soon after that. It is a wretched thing for parents and babies but it will be grown out of and will not remain a permanent block to getting to sleep.

NAPPIES AND CLOTHING

The comfort of nappies and clothing is something to check very carefully. If you use towelling nappies make sure they are very soft. Rinse out every trace of washing powder and use a fabric conditioner. For disposable users make sure you buy the brand that best suits the baby's shape and size and that doesn't feel to you too sharp-edged and 'crunchy'. Take care too that you never stick the little tabs to any of his skin by mistake. His vest too must feel nice and soft – babies' skin is very delicate and can be chafed uncomfortably very easily. Check baby's pyjamas, night-dress or Babygro for roughness, tightness, rubbing labels and so on – remember there's no way that the baby can tell you what may be bothering him. When I was about $1\frac{1}{2}$ my father apparently spent a whole day with me grizzling and complaining inarticulately only to discover at bedtime that he had put both of my legs through one hole in my knickers when dressing me that morning.

NAPPY RASH

This can be a common cause of wakefulness. If it's bad you must consult your doctor or health visitor as it may be caused by something needing specific treatment, but there are some things

'The heartbeat that the baby would have heard while still inside.'

you can do to avoid the common rashes. Change the nappy as frequently as possible and always as soon as the baby has passed a stool. Use a disposable one-way liner which will help to keep the skin dry. Leave the nappy off as much as possible to let air get to the skin. Clean the skin thoroughly every time you change him but preferably not with soap and water as they can be very drying. I find Milguard very good indeed. If you use that then you will not need anything else but if you clean with a simple baby lotion then rub in a little protective cream afterwards. Don't use plastic pants if there is any hint of soreness. At any sign of a rash apply plenty of one of the many special creams. If it doesn't improve very quickly then consult your doctor and work hard together to get rid of it — a baby with a sore bottom is naturally going to be unhappy and unable to sleep well.

Breast-fed babies are less likely than bottle-fed to get nappy rash but they are in no way immune to it. Especially when you start to introduce solids and the stools change you must be prepared for the possibility of a reaction in the skin around his bottom.

Most of the disposable nappies are whitened with a chemical which may possibly cause a reaction in the skin of certain babies and it's a good idea to try one of the brands that are not treated in this way. Some are also perfumed and 'sanitised'. Both perfume and antiseptic can cause problems in some babies. Peau Douce is one type which is free from any bleach or chemical.

If he gets very wet at night and you don't want to have to keep waking him up to change him then slip an extra disposable pad inside his usual nappy.

Most babies dislike being left in a messy nappy so if he passes a stool in the middle of the night you will have to change him. With any luck his body will adapt fairly quickly to a daytime pattern and at night the nappies will be only wet.

ECZEMA

Another type of rash that is quite often found in babies is infantile eczema. This can cause very bad itching and keep the poor baby awake. Of course you will consult your doctor immediately if you find any patches and follow whatever treatment he prescribes. I found old-fashioned coal tar paste remarkably effective on Alexander. One comfort is that this type of eczema is usually grown out of by the time the child is two.

COLDS

Colds are also frequently causes of difficulty in sleeping, particularly in a British winter. If the baby's nose gets very blocked up he may be unable to feed. This will distress him and make him cry, which in turn will make his nose even worse and you are into a difficult vicious circle. Your doctor may prescribe nose drops to use before feeding, but of course you should avoid using them for any length of time. Try a Wright's inhaler in the room. If he tends to get a cough whenever he gets a cold then it may be worth buying a humidifier. The most effective but expensive kind are those that puff out a stream of hot steam – the modern equivalent of holding the baby near a boiling kettle or running shower. If you suspect that the baby has a temperature or may have pain in his ears or throat then you must seek medical help quickly as an infection must be dealt with straight away. Ear trouble seems to be unfortunately only too common in young children but as long as it is attended to correctly it is something they will grow out of without being left with any damage. Make sure he is not getting either too hot or too cold in the night – see pp. 36, 39, 41 for suggestions for bedding, clothes and room temperature.

TEETHING

The pain of teething seems to affect babies in very different ways – some sail through the whole business unscathed while others have a very miserable time. It is dangerous to blame too much on teething, and you should always check with the doctor if there is any fever, ear-rubbing or bad nappy rash – just three of the many symptoms that some mothers remain convinced are part of the normal teething process. However it can make the gums very sore, and cause extra dribbling which in turn may produce a rash around the mouth and it is a very common cause of waking in the night.

There are various remedies you can try, one of which may work for your particular baby. There are jellies and lotions to rub on the sore gum with your finger which do help to numb the area temporarily and may relieve the pain long enough for the baby to be able to get back to sleep. Be wary of using these too much as they contain local anaesthetics which can occasionally cause allergies, and some of them also contain aspirin. They appear to taste delicious – Katie was a real Bonjela freak and even now will

use every excuse to be allowed to use it. I never realised the second set of teeth coming through could cause such problems ... An old remedy is simply firm and rhythmical rubbing with the thumb or finger while the baby is being cuddled. Not so good at night – though if Mum or Dad is awake anyway they might as well do it. A teething ring or very hard biscuit to bite on may bring relief, but of course only use them while you are there – never leave the baby alone in his cot with something in his mouth. Put things that he likes to bite on in the fridge – often the coldness can bring a little extra relief.

Some of the homeopathic and herbal remedies are safely worth a try – for instance there is a camomile preparation that you rub onto the gums and tongue which is said to bring relief.

If the teething is very bad then a little junior aspirin or paracetamol may be necessary to relieve the pain – but remember there will be lots of teething to come and you don't want to be reaching for the aspirin bottle every time it appears.

Older babies may continue to wake in the night even once the teething bout is over, and you may have to gently break them of the habit. (p. 72)

MEDICINES

As a general rule I am against the use of medicines to help a baby sleep except in very special circumstances but obviously if the baby is unwell there may be a need for their use. The golden rule is never to give any form of medicine without medical advice. If he has an itchy condition such as eczema or urticaria then the doctor may prescribe a mild sedative to help him sleep, usually an antihistamine. Naturally this should be used for as short a time as possible. If he is in pain or running a temperature then on your doctor's advice you may need to give him a little junior aspirin or paracetamol. If he is prescribed an antibiotic to combat an infection then do make sure he finishes the complete course.

Some medicines unfortunately taste really disgusting, and the sweet flavourings used in an attempt to mask them don't always help. Alexander recently had to undergo a course of antibiotics for an ear infection and took violently against the bright pink liquid containing it. Getting him to take it three times a day became a battle, and heartrending for us to have to administer it to a protesting but still polite two year old screaming 'No thank you' as we approached him with the spoon. Still of course it was worth it in the end to see him free of the ear-rubbing misery he had been in.

There has been much interest in alternative medicine in recent years, and there are homeopathic and herbal remedies that can safely be tried.

OLDER BABIES AND TODDLERS

Much of the preceding chapters will apply to all ages of baby, but there are also additional and very different problems and solutions that arise once the baby has dropped his night feeds and begins to grow into more of an independent person.

FEEDING

The age at which he will stop waking from hunger will vary considerably. Some wonderful morning you may wake up and realize with amazement that you have slept right through the night: it can be quite a startling experience – the first time Katie slept right through I woke in a panic thinking something was wrong. Don't however be fooled into thinking the baby will never wake in the night again – often you get one or two good nights followed by a bad one again. With luck the good ones will become more frequent until it is rare to be woken for a feed.

If this happy course of events doesn't happen naturally then there are one or two ways of trying to encourage it. If you find that you are being regularly woken an hour or so after you get into bed then it may be worth waking the baby for a feed just before you go to sleep. At least then you will get the full benefit of the next stretch between feeds, and with any luck he will go that bit longer than he would have otherwise as he will be completely topped up. If you are convinced that he is waking in the night more from habit than from hunger then it may be worth giving him warm boiled water instead of his feed – with some babies after a few nights this seems to persuade them that it is not worth their while waking up. It's probably better if Dad goes to him at night if you are trying to drop a feed – the smell of milk on the mother may remind him of feeding when he doesn't really need it.

Follow the advice in the feeding chapter on making the night feeds as quick, boring and uneventful as possible.

If he still continues to wake, take a feed and go back to sleep again, then just accept the fact that he still needs it, and count yourself lucky that at least you still have an easy way of getting him quickly back to sleep. Naturally fed babies may go on taking feeds at night well into their second years and you should never feel that you are in any way doing something wrong or 'spoiling' them by continuing to give it to them.

BEDTIME

The older the baby gets the more important routine becomes in helping him to settle happily to sleep. If from an early age it is an accepted fact of life that at a certain time each evening he will have a bath followed by some quiet play and then be tucked up in bed for a few songs and then a goodnight kiss or whatever ritual may have evolved, it will be much easier for him to feel secure about being left to go to sleep. There will come a time of course in many toddlers' lives when they suddenly realise that they don't after all have to do everything you say without question and there are bound to be some protests about bed at some point. Alexander can produce some magnificent tantrums and as he's a big strong baby we have sometimes had to go through some ferocious wrestling matches on the way up to bed. I suppose I like to think of myself as a peace-loving liberal and it's quite startling to have produced a little creature who can turn into an aggressive furious monster hurling heartfelt if limited epithets at his devoted mother. Having been through that a few times though he soon found it didn't cut any ice and he's now very happy to go to bed each evening. Katie used to protest on occasions just as violently in her own way, but at least it was more vocally than physically.

Of course in times of illness or on a special occasion such as a birthday or visit from a grandparent the rules will be broken, but on the whole the more the bedtime routine can be stuck to the happier everyone will be.

Never never use bed as a threat during the day. You can't expect him to go happily up to his bedroom at night if he has been told he'll be 'sent to bed' when doing something naughty.

If as a small baby he has always dropped off to sleep while feeding you may have to gently and gradually teach him to fall asleep in his cot. Try some of the ideas on pp. 42–60. If you find you are spending hours every night singing, rocking or patting then a consistent programme of kind re-training may be necessary.

As soon as possible you want to get into the habit of leaving the room with him still awake but happy, rather than hovering around waiting for him to fall asleep. Talk about a watched pot never boiling – my husband and I between us must have spent countless hours sitting next to Katie's cot watching her eyelids droop into apparent slumber over and over again. It's amazing how long children can fight sleep when they really want to. My Uncle Harry had a theory that by standing at the head of the cot instead of the side he could make my cousin drop off more quickly – the strain of tilting the head up and back to look at his father would help the eyes to close sooner. No success guaranteed but an interesting idea.

Check the room for any pictures or objects that may look 'spooky' in the half dark and be worrying the child into staying awake – coats on backs of doors, paintings with faces in and so on. Beware of this being played on once they can talk: my little niece Sarah would keep her father in the bedroom for hours by calling him back over and over again as she found new things that were 'worrying' her – 'Oh and Daddy that picture there ... and I think that book on the table looks a bit funny ... and those curtains are rather strange ...' she practically had the room cleared each night until Dad put his foot down.

Don't make the change from day to night too sudden – try to wind down the excitement level gradually to aim towards a calm bedtime. Make the late afternoon games gentle ones, and try to avoid confrontation in the pre-bed hours. It's worth ignoring small misdemeanours rather than end the day with a row. A warm drink of milk can sometimes help to make him sleepy. Put it in a bottle if he still enjoys the comfort of sucking.

Once he's in bed and you have finished the ritual, try pottering about where he can still hear you, tidying up or putting out his clothes for the next day and perhaps even quietly chatting to him while you do it, until you casually mention that you're going downstairs now or into the kitchen to make Daddy's supper etc.

One evening when I wasn't feeling very well I told Alexander as I left the room that I was going to put on my night things and get ready for bed. He happened to go off to sleep very easily and peacefully and so I said it again the next night and the next until I found myself in the ludicrous position of having to put a dressing gown over my clothes each evening when I went back to tuck him in so as not to be caught out if he should wake.

My niece used to go to sleep happily if my sister said she was just 'popping to the loo', so every night for months that's what she said. Little Helen must surely have wondered why on earth her mother never remembered to go before she put her to bed.

Don't let it always be the same parent that puts him to bed – it will make life much easier if from an early age either Dad or Mum can do the bedtime routine.

Never be tempted to get the baby out of the cot or you will find it very difficult to get him back again and he will bully you every evening until you get him out.

By now he may well have adopted a comfort object, whether it's a favourite toy, blanket or a dummy or just a well-sucked thumb: many children use such things as an indispensable part of their night-time routine. Never try to discourage this – it's all part of the process of learning to comfort himself to sleep without your presence, and research show that children who have such habits have far fewer problems with getting to sleep than those without. If you can engineer it so that the chosen object is easily duplicated then you may save yourself a lot of

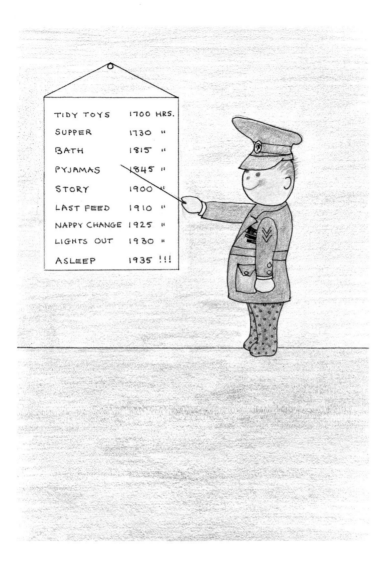

'The older the baby gets the more important routine becomes.'

trouble later. Many parents have spent frantic evenings searching for some beloved one-eared moth-eaten bunny without which the protesting toddler adamantly refuses to go to sleep. Put a couple of books or safe toys in the cot that he can play with on his own before he goes to sleep.

If in spite of all this careful preparation for sleep he still cries when you leave the room then wait a few minutes, go back, give him another kiss and cuddle, tuck him up again, say goodnight firmly and *leave*. You may have to repeat this over and over again the first few nights, but as long as you keep going back as cheerfully as possible he will eventually realise that you are never far away and that you are not leaving him for ever and he will settle to sleep. He may scream and shout each time you leave the room but if you keep calm and go back each time after a few minutes then it will be more out of anger than distress. Never leave him unhappy for long — five minutes is the absolute maximum, and never give in and take him out of the cot or you will be going right back to square one. This may well take an hour or more of going in every few minutes but if you don't weaken it will eventually work and after two or three days will get shorter and shorter. I believe a toddler likes the security of knowing you will stick to what you say as long as it is done kindly. If he has got into the habit of a prolonged bedtime with you staying in the room until he is asleep then be sure to set aside a few free evenings to begin your new routine, as if you are worrying about cooking the supper or getting on with something downstairs it will make it much harder for you to spend much of the evening going in and out of his room every five minutes without getting very tense.

Never leave him to cry alone in his cot for long — even if it eventually 'trains' him to go to sleep on his own you will have put him through some extremely lonely and unhappy times and taught him that he is right to feel insecure about your love and attention.

If he is a child who needs very little sleep then you may have to keep him up all evening until you go to bed. This is the standard practice in many parts of the world; we are in the minority in expecting to have child-free evenings. I must say I rather value them – they seem to be the only times my husband and I manage to sustain uninterrupted conversations.

DAY BEFORE

It is very unfair to expect a baby to go happily to sleep at night if he is just not tired, and it is up to you to make sure that he has had the right amount of daytime activity and sleep to suit his particular needs, and to leave him tired enough to sleep but not overtired. Make his days as enjoyably exhausting as possible – include active physical exercise, preferably in the fresh air, as well as plenty of intellectual stimulation.

As he gets older you will have to become more aware of how much sleep your particular baby needs and adjust his daytime naps so that he is tired enough at night. Babies vary so much in the amount they need that it is impossible to give a set pattern but at some stage you will notice that the haphazard routine of the early days will settle into a morning and afternoon sleep. If necessary you will have to wake him from the afternoon one early enough for him to be ready for bed later on. Never let him drop off in the late afternoon – it may be tempting after a long demanding day to get a few minutes peace, particularly as this can be the most fractious time, but you will regret it later. Keep him awake by any means possible so that he will be ready for a peaceful bedtime and a good night's sleep. A walk in the pram or buggy or a drive in the car too late in the day may be fatal – many's the time I've had to lift a drowsy child out of the buggy and carry it home on one arm chatting or making silly faces at it in order to keep it awake, with the other arm trying to manage buggy, shopping and an irritable eight year old.

There will come an awkward stage when two daytime naps are too much and one is not quite enough. You will just have to play it by ear – letting him have the two rests when he is really tired and then perhaps managing two or three days with only one. The pattern will be entirely an individual one and only you can judge how much sleep he needs during the day without spoiling his nights.

Whatever pattern of daytime sleep you find he needs, stick to it. Don't be tempted to let him sleep on in the afternoon for instance if you know he has had enough; wake him gently. Alexander always woke in the most terrible mood from his afternoon nap and the rest of the family had to steel itself for the onslaught of 'Yuk' 'Go away' 'You're horrible' etc. etc. with which the waker would be greeted (his early grasp of language did have its disadvantages) but we knew the penalty of leaving him to sleep peacefully on would have to be paid later.

Eventually he will be ready to drop the daytime sleep altogether but be prepared for him to need it occasionally, especially after a particularly active morning or when he has been ill. Once he starts playgroup or nursery school he may return to an after lunch snooze on a regular basis for a while.

Don't try to make him drop the daytime sleep too early by forcing him to stay awake all day long – you might think that it will make him so tired that he will sleep better at night but it just doesn't work that way. Overtiredness is just as destructive to good peaceful sleep as not being tired enough. There have been several occasions when I have let one of the children have a longer and later nap during the day than I intended and have anticipated a difficult bedtime and wakeful night only to be taken quite unawares by one of the longest and quietest nights ever. You can never safely predict which will be the perfect amount of sleep during the day, but on the whole you can normally judge it fairly well.

Once the daytime sleep has been dropped on a fairly regular basis you may find he needs an earlier bedtime to compensate. The thought of an extra hour without his company in the evening may not fill you with too much dismay now that you are looking after him all day without the accustomed break while he sleeps....

Try to avoid any stressful situations during the day until his

'Try to avoid confrontation in the pre-bed hours.'

sleeping is more consistent. Any major change in his life may well be reflected in his night-time behaviour. You may find yourself delaying moving house until he's in his twenties. . . .

Travelling with a child who sleeps badly can be very difficult, but equally they can sometimes surprise you with their reactions: occasionally a change of scene seems to throw them into a better sleeping pattern. A friend of mine had a sleepless child who slept through the night for the first time on a visit to America – the jet-lag seemed to take her so by surprise that it mixed up her whole schedule and re-set it into a much calmer and longer-sleeping one. It continued after they returned home. Unfortunately it would be somewhat impractical and expensive to send sleepless children off to America on the National Health, but it does illustrate just how complicated and unpredictable the whole business is.

Try to see that he eats well during the day so that he will not wake in the night through hunger. As with little babies it's more a question of his input taken as a whole than a large late meal just before bed.

Avoid stories or television programmes that may inspire bad dreams, often the cause of a child's waking at night. It's sometimes difficult to foretell what may be the cause of worrying thoughts but if you do get a hint that something may upset him then don't try to jolly him out of it – the fear may seem quite irrational to you but it is very real to him, and if he feels you don't understand he may keep it hidden inside where it may easily emerge in nightmares.

WAKING IN THE NIGHT

Once the baby is no longer waking to be fed in the night then of course you hope that he will consistently sleep right through. Unfortunately this is frequently not the case, and the toddler who still wakes his parents two or three times in the night is far more common than many people think.

Most babies wake in the night several times, but it depends what they do when they wake as to whether it is seen as a problem. If they turn over and go straight back to sleep then of course no one will even be aware that they have woken. If on the other hand they cry for company and refuse to go back to sleep for several hours then it can become a very real problem indeed.

First check for any physical discomfort that may be waking him – see 'Discomfort'. If he kicks off his coverings in the night and gets cold then put him into one of the cosy all-in-one sleep

suits, or fix the bedclothes with clips to the rails and the cot. Alexander always slept better if I turned his duvet sideways and tucked it firmly round him under the mattress – acting perhaps as a sort of toddler-swaddling as well as keeping him warm. If necessary put a heater in the room in very cold weather. If you think he gets too hot then put him in thinner nightwear or leave more of the window open; there is much less danger from getting too cold once the baby is six months or so.

Make sure the room is neither too light nor too dark – fear of the dark is very real and should not be dismissed or laughed at. If you live in an old creaky house as we do then you will need to work out the most silent route for entering and leaving the baby's room in the night. If he is waking just as you go to bed each evening then consider whether you are making unnecessary noise that may be disturbing him – during shallow periods of sleep even a distant loo-flush may get through to him. Do you have central heating that is on an automatic timer that may be making a noise as it switches itself off?

If you have checked for all physical causes but he still continues to wake in the night then it is obviously for some less easily solved reason. I have never been able to leave a baby or child crying on his own in the night – if it eventually did stop him calling I've always felt it would have been a battle won at far too high a price. On the other hand some parents find that ignoring their babies' cries in the night for a few days can quickly break a habit of waking. If you and the neighbours can stand it it may be something to try if you're desperate and is certainly nothing to feel guilty about. If you're not prepared to ignore him then one solution in the middle of the night is to bring him into your bed. This will give him the security and comfort he is after and may give all of you the chance to get quickly back to sleep. The trouble is that once you start doing it it will be very difficult to stop again without causing much misery, so unless you are prepared to have him sleeping in the bed with you for quite some time to come then it's probably best avoided. Also some toddlers turn into windmills as soon as they hit the sheet, or else manage to produce more extraordinary variations on the sound of breathing than you would think possible from such tiny noses and mouths. (See p. 30 for more on the family bed.) There will be times when he is unwell when you will naturally want to bring him into bed for a cuddle but unless it is to become a regular habit then once he is better you must make it clear that it is time to go back into his own bed.

A compromise is to bring his cot into your bedroom. You may find that he sleeps much better knowing that you are near all night, and even if he does wake then you may be able to calm him merely by the sound of your voice.

Alternatively you can put a camp bed temporarily in his bedroom so that if necessary you can spend the night in his room. This means that at least one parent will get a good night's sleep and if you put the extra bed right next to the cot then a reassuring pat may be enough to quieten him. If you have other children in the family then you could try putting the toddler in with them. You might think that they would all end up waking, but surprisingly enough this doesn't usually happen, and quite

'By now he may well have adopted a comfort object.'

often the feeling of there being someone else in the room helps the wakeful one to sleep through. After all most humans in the world even today sleep with their young and we are unusual in expecting them to sleep alone.

Unless he is ill or extremely upset by some event of the day then it's not a good idea to take him out of his cot and bring him downstairs or into your sitting room. We made the mistake of doing just that with Alexander, who soon got into the habit of regular 4.30 am games and fun. It took a long time to break him of the habit and would have been much better never started in the first place. The 'cure' consisted of sitting with him in the early hours kindly but firmly refusing to take him out of the cot. He did get very upset but I felt that as long as one of us was with him, usually holding him in a tight cuddle and singing or chatting to him while still in the cot, he would not feel any loneliness or real distress. After a lot of protests he would eventually lie down and then after a goodnight kiss and a tuck-in we would leave the room. This sequence had to be repeated a few times for the first two or three nights, but he then learnt that it was a waste of time to keep it up and accepted that he was to be in the cot all night.

If he wakes and you don't want to start playing musical beds then go to him straight away, reassure him, kiss him goodnight and *leave*. If he cries go back after a minute or two and repeat this, being kind and loving but firmly letting him know that night is for sleeping and that you're not going to get involved in any long sessions with him. Consistency and firmness are vital. You may have to repeat this several times for a few nights but he will eventually realise that you mean what you say and thereafter even if he does wake he will probably go quickly back to sleep again.

If he's thirsty give him water — not sweet interesting drinks.

Be firm but kind in the night; try not to lose your temper with him but equally don't get involved in long rocking or singing sessions or you will be doing it every night.

If he climbs out of the cot then take him firmly back and settle him down again. The more quickly you do this the better, so that he learns it's not worth his while to try. If you have always responded quickly to his cries then he may never have tried this anyway.

Some children will play happily on their own in the night if they wake — you could try putting a couple of safe toys or books in the corner of his cot. If he always wants a drink when he wakes then a beaker with a lid could also be put in the corner of the cot; he might just learn to help himself without disturbing you.

Something well worth trying if a consistent pattern of night waking exists is to get someone else to put the baby to bed for a few days. With several wakeful toddlers I know this had quite a dramatic effect on their sleeping. It's probably best if the parent who usually puts them to bed actually leaves the house as if to go out — or even goes away for a few days — leaving the toddler with the other parent or someone else that he trusts. This very often stops them waking: it's as if they sense that it's not worth their while calling as Mum/Dad isn't there. A few days of this may set a new pattern.

Sometimes star charts used in the morning can be effective — let him stick on his own star every time he sleeps right through the night. This is know by behavioural psychologists as 'reinforcement', in other words when they do something good something nice happens. It's a new name for a very old technique for dealing with people – bribery – and one to which most of us invariably resort.

If he wakes with what they call night-terrors then there's nothing you can do but help him through them. Katie occasionally had them. They are different from nightmares in that the child is neither asleep nor fully awake, but in a strange confused state of fear which may take a few minutes to subside. You can't really get through to him and it's best just to cuddle him and talk reassuringly until it's over.

The same method of dealing with them applies to nightmares, but it's worth thinking through the events of the preceding day or so to discover any obvious cause – a frightening programme on television or an over realistic game of monsters perhaps. There may be some problem or change in his life which is making him insecure. Children can be anxious over apparently minor problems that nevertheless are overwhelmingly important to them. You may need to gently wake him from his nightmare before he can allow himself to get back to peaceful sleep.

Never leave a child alone with a night-terror or nightmare. He is not 'playing you up' but needs you to calm him. Let him have a light left on in the room if it reassures him, or a door left ajar with a light on the landing.

WAKING EARLY

Waking early when you have a baby becomes part of your life, but it all depends what you mean by early as to whether you find it bearable or not. To us after three early risers anything after 6.0 is tolerable, after 7.0 very reasonable and after 8.0 unimaginable luxury.

Parents of young children are in a strange category all of their own when it comes to the twice yearly British time changes, reacting in quite the opposite way to the rest of the population. When the clocks go forward for summertime for most 'normal' people it means they are deprived of an hour's sleep: for you and me it means the baby will be waking – oh joy! – at 6.30 rather than 5.30 ... And at the return of Greenwich mean time when most people enjoy an extra hour in bed we can only look forward to baby's return to waking at some unearthly hour.

There are ways of trying to give yourself a few extra precious minutes:

If light is waking him in the summertime put up heavier curtains or line the present ones with dark material.

As long as he sleeps within earshot then put a beaker of drink and a rusk next to the cot where he can reach them. With these plus a couple of interesting toys he might amuse himself for a little while.

If a wet or messy nappy wakes him you might find after a change and a cuddle he will play on his own and let you go back to bed for a bit.

If there is an older child in the family let him go to the baby when he wakes. They may easily learn to keep each other company in the mornings.

Make sure you're not putting him to bed too early – it may be preferable to have his company for a little longer in the evenings to being woken horribly early.

Take it in turns with your husband to be the one to go to him in the mornings, so that at least one parent will have a lie-in.

Try to see things through your child's eyes: it can sometimes be very difficult to guess what may be affecting them. One little boy I knew having always been happy to play in his cot in the early mornings suddenly started getting very upset when he woke. The parents went through everything that might be worrying him, clearing the room of everything he might see first thing that could be causing his distress. It wasn't for a long time that they realised that on the mantlepiece was a postcard from Wales: on the postcard was a stamp: on the stamp was a dragon!

Make the most of early morning television – sometimes even the news and weather can be fascinating enough for a baby for you to be able to doze off for a few moments on the sofa. I must say though that there is something rather depressing about finding yourself waiting impatiently for Frank Bough or Nick Owen at 6.15 in the morning. Sundays are wonderful of course, when one is given a full hour of relief by 'Rub-a-dub-tub'.

Finally, accept early waking as another of those aspects of parenthood that are regrettable but unavoidable; try to get to bed at a reasonable hour while the phase lasts and above all enjoy your lively loving baby at what can be one of their most charming times – all warm, sleepy and tousled and ready to give you a heart-melting smile. (Except our Alexander, who tends to wake up unbelievably grumpy and ready for battle, and like many adults has to be handled very tactfully for the first few minutes. The aim is to avoid all confrontation until he has had his cornflakes, after which he begins to be more like his usual jolly self.)

HOW TO COPE

A sleepless baby can disrupt the entire household. Particularly of course one or both of the parents will suffer, as lack of sleep in itself is extremely debilitating, quite apart from the trauma of pacing the floor with a wakeful, crying baby. It is very important that you think of yourself and your partner occasionally and that you don't let the baby entirely dominate your lives. Hopefully both mother and father will be equally involved in every aspect of looking after the baby and love and support for each other can be vital during these difficult nights.

There is a natural tendency in the middle of the night to blame someone or something for one's lack of sleep, and as your husband or wife is usually the person within firing range the most enormous amount of resentment can be built up. I've known nights when we've been up with one of the babies when I've so much wanted to shout at someone that I've almost unconsciously tried to engineer a situation where a row could be started. In our house we have always shared the night vigils as equally as breastfeeding will allow but it obviously makes sense to take it in turns to a certain extent so that at least one of you gets some sleep. In spite of the logic of there being no point in two of you being kept awake there is something supremely irritating about a snoring spouse lying in bed while mother or father paces the floor with the baby. It can be one of the loneliest times of all, and at three in the morning when you are at your lowest ebb you can begin to feel the whole world is against you.

My sister used to keep a diary of her bad nights with her daughter – she found it helped to write down some of the despairing thoughts she used to have. Part of the trouble is that as well as the awful tiredness and unhappiness you can feel enormous guilt: here you are with a healthy baby complaining about something as trivial as lack of sleep. It certainly isn't trivial at the time, and anyone who has gone through years of being woken regularly at night from deep sleep possibly to be kept up for hours at a stretch will know just what an insidious form of torture it can be.

Probably the most important thing to remember is that it will pass. It's hard to realise it but there will come a time when the children will all sleep through the night and will even resent you getting them up in the morning, and the more love and attention you have given them in the early years, particularly at night, the more loving and secure people they will themselves grow up to be. If you think of every time you go to them at night as a sort of premium in an insurance policy which will pay out for the whole of their adult lives then it makes it easier to bear.

As you've crept out of the room after apparently settling your little angel for the twelfth time and he screams for Mummy or Daddy just as you are finally sitting down to your dried-up luke warm supper, try to keep any unavoidable swearing out of his earshot. Many's the time I've muttered the most hideous oaths silently to myself as I return for the umpteenth time to the baby's room, and it takes the performance of a lifetime to enter sweetly and lovingly once more into the monster's lair.

Parents whose children sleep through the night from an early age are very lucky, but you must never let them make you feel that the fact that yours still wake in the night at the age of two or three is in any way your fault or anything particularly unusual. More than 20% of babies are still waking regularly at a year old or beyond There is evidence to show that the type of alert, wakeful infant that doesn't sleep through the night for a long time will have been in some way programmed to be so since birth, or even from mid-pregnancy, so there is no reason to suppose that it is due to your handling of him.

Some people simply ignore their babies' crying at night and feel proud of the fact that this successfully 'trains' them to sleep through, but if you can't do this then you must remain firm in

'You could try putting books in the corner of his cot.'

your conviction that a crying child needs you and that you are right to go to him.

There are some ways of lessening the burden. Try to have an evening out together from time to time – perhaps book a babysitter for a few days ahead to give you something to work towards. If breastfeeding then start expressing milk a few days ahead and storing it in the freezer to make sure you have built up enough supplies for the evening out so that you won't be anxious (p. 16). If you have difficulty getting a reliable babysitter you might be able to swap evenings with a couple who also have a young baby, by them bringing their baby to your house in a carrycot for the evening and then you doing the same for them on a later occasion.

If you are breastfeeding then once you get into the habit of expressing milk it can be very helpful in enabling you to get some rest. Let your husband do a couple of nights with expressed milk in a bottle for the baby while you sleep – but make sure you're in a room far enough away not to be able to hear him, or you will be half listening all night. Leave a bottle with someone during the day occasionally, so that you can go out with a friend or even just take the opportunity to do a little quiet shopping on your own. Don't forget the leakage problem if you're out when you would normally be feeding. I couldn't find any breast pads in the house the other evening and went rushing out to the first night of *Starlight Express* with one-way nappy liners stuffed down my bra. They seemed to do the trick luckily.

Get to know other parents of young babies by going to local playgroups, mother and baby groups, one o'clock clubs etc. It can be very comforting to know just how normal it is for babies to wake at night, and it's always a welcome relief to talk about it.

Don't hesitate to use a dummy if it helps the family to get a few hours precious sleep (p. 47). Ignore people who make you feel guilty by showing their disapproval.

Bring the baby into your bed whenever it feels right to do so; it is a very natural thing to do and far more commonly practised in Britain than many people let on (p. 28).

Accept the fact that sleep will be in short bursts rather than the long stretches you are used to. After you have fed the baby each time and settled him try to relax yourself so that you can get back to sleep as quickly as possible. Don't lie there straining to catch every sound the baby makes – if he does need you he'll soon let you know, and if he doesn't then you're wasting valuable sleep time. On the other hand if you're having difficulty getting back to sleep don't get too wound up about it – it's not the end of the world and you can survive on a remarkably small amount of sleep. Try to lie there thinking about something pleasant – we are often comfortingly told that these wakeful babies are likely to be very bright children: picture the little darling top of his class and imagine how proud you'll be. . . .

Don't worry about anything in the middle of the night – everything really will seem different in the morning. Put off any serious thinking until you are in a better mood; any decision you make at 3 am in the morning will almost certainly have to be re-thought out the next day.

Remember you're not the only parent who has spent several months walking around all day like a zombie – you will survive this lack of sleep and even get used to the strange light-headed feeling it gives you.

Do get your partner or a relative or friend to take over the baby for a couple of hours during the day when you get really overtired so that you can catch up on some sleep. Don't be tempted to use the time to do all those things you've been unable to do with a demanding baby around – go straight to bed and SLEEP! Remember once you've slept, everything will seem much more possible and you'll have twice the energy.

Don't blame your partner or the poor baby in the middle of the night.

Suspend all judgements on anything until the morning – write down any bad thoughts you have, it's a good way of getting them out of your system. There's no point in two of you being awake so if you are breastfeeding you do the nights and let your partner take over the baby at some point during the day so that you can catch up.

Make yourself sleep during the day whenever the baby does.

SINGLE PARENTS

I have assumed throughout the book that both parents will be sharing in every aspect of looking after the baby including the difficult nights. There are of course many mothers and fathers who either through choice or force of circumstances are bringing up babies on their own, or who have a partner unwilling to share the responsibilities and problems that having a family brings.

If you have any relatives that may be willing to help then don't be afraid to ask them – it can be quite flattering to be needed, and often grandparents or uncles or aunts like to show off how well they can handle a baby. Our society makes it very difficult to bring up a child on your own as our families are frequently so split up and dispersed unlike the old days of close communities.

Make sure you go to your local clinic regularly, and ask your health visitor about any particular problems with sleeping that you may have. You are bound to meet other parents of young children while you are there – try to get chatting to them as it can be enormously helpful to have someone to talk to, and if you become friendly you may be able to help each other with baby-sitting later.

Don't feel you're alone in having terrible nights and some miserable days; it's almost certainly not your fault that the baby doesn't sleep well.

Bring him into your bed if it helps you both to sleep – you may well enjoy each other's company, and at least you don't have a jealous partner to cope with!

USEFUL ADDRESSES

Mothercare
(Branches nationwide)
Excellent for everything for mothers and babies. I tried out
several of their products while writing the book, and can
particularly recommend the following:
De-luxe baby carrier
Lightweight PVC carrycot
Three-way adjustable height dropside cot
Swinging crib
Swingomatic (wind-up baby swing)
Travel cot
Super sitter system
Baby alarm
Convector heater
Reclining baby car seat
Bouncing cradle
Baby walker
Their range of babystretch suits and baby bags is also very
good.

Winganna Natural Products Sandy Hill Enterprises, Sandy
Hill Cottage, Sandy Haven, St Ishmaels, Haverfordwest,
Dyfed SA62 3DL
Tel. Dale (06465) 403
For natural baby fleeces (lambskins) and other products.

Mr and Mrs Howard Owens
Lullababy, Leominster HR6 9BR
Tel. 054 47 630
For the Lullababy vertical rocker and other products.

Farley Health Products Ltd.
Torr Lane, Plymouth, Devon.
Can supply videos on such subjects as 'crying', 'sleeping' etc.

Hushabye Baby Products
c/o Diss Handling Centre, Diss, Northants
For 'womb music'.

The British Homeopathic Association
27a, Devonshire Street, London, WIN IRJ

The Family Welfare Association
501–505, Kingsland Road, London, E8 4AU.

Hyperactive Children's Support Group
59, Meadowside, Angmering, Sussex BN16 4BW.

The National Childbirth Trust
9, Queensborough Terrace, Bayswater, London, W2 3TB.
Tel. 01-221 3833
For hiring of electrical breast-pumps and many other helpful
services.

Toy Libraries Association
Seabrook House, Wyllyotts Manor, Darkes Lane, Potters Bar,
Herts EN6 2HL

The Herb Society
34, Boscobel Place, London, SW1
Tel. 01-235 1530

Kangol A.S.E. UK Ltd.
Norfolk Street, Carlisle CA2 5HX.
Tel. 0228 31711
For the 'Dreamseat' reclining baby car seat and other car
safety products.